SHE IN THE SHADOWS

SPY IN THE SHADOWS

by Barbara Greenwood

Happy Reading, Paul

Barbara Greenwood

KIDS CAN PRESS LTD.
TORONTO

Kids Can Press Ltd. acknowledges with appreciation the assistance of the Canada Council and the Ontario Arts Council in the production of this book.

Canadian Cataloguing in Publication Data

Greenwood, Barbara, 1940-
    Spy in the shadows

ISBN 1-55074-018-0

I. Title.

PS8563.R43S78 1990   jC813'.54   C90-094340-8
PZ7.G74Sp 1990

Kids Can Press Ltd.
585½ Bloor Street West
Toronto, Ontario, Canada
M6G 1K5

Edited by Charis Wahl
Designed by N.R. Jackson
Typeset by Pixel Graphics Inc.
Printed and bound in Canada by Webcom Ltd.

90 0 9 8 7 6 5 4 3 2 1

In memory of my parents
George and Anne Auer
one, a master craftsman
the other, the Irish presence in my life.

ACKNOWLEDGEMENTS

Historical novels contain facts that must be checked and rechecked. For constant and diligent historical detective work, I thank my husband, Robert E. Greenwood. And for asking the right questions at the right time, while I was struggling to shape and polish the manuscript, I thank my editor, Charis Wahl.

THE PARTS OF A BELL

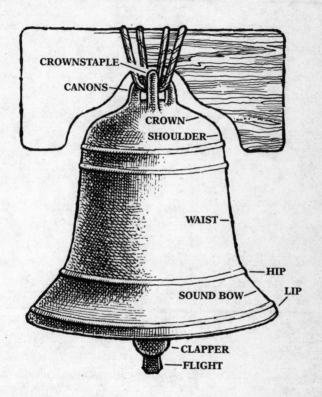

CHAPTER

ONE

Liam knelt on the cold, earthen floor gazing at the bell on his outstretched palm. I've done it! What do you think of that, Da? I've done it! My first pour. If only I could show you. He had to swallow the lump that still caught him unawares. Don't spoil it, he ordered himself and jumped up to carry the bell over to the foundry windows.

He held it to the light, inspecting it as though he were the master founder himself. Mottled grey like every fresh casting he'd seen in his year at the foundry. Polish it up, he thought, turning it slowly in the fading afternoon light, and it's perfect. Perfect! He could almost hear

Gottlieb Hahn. A good bell, my boy. A job well done. This time, this time for sure he'll say that.

He ran his thumb over the flaring hip and across the sound bow. Tiny jagged points pricked his skin. He peered closely at the scattering of rough blisters along the metal surface. "Polishing," he said out loud. "Just a bit of polishing. That's all it needs." He set the bell on the workbench and turned to the wooden casing that held the rest of his pour. The sand was dry and cool now. As he dug the second bell out of the mould, he pictured himself showing off all six when the founder returned. What do you think of that, Master Hahn? And you said I wasn't ready yet!

What next? Oh, yes, the ring. How he loved that moment when a bell's first note quivered in the air — like the hum of his father's tuning fork. One second silence, the next a shimmer of perfect tone. He picked up Gottlieb's tiny mallet, took a deep breath, and tapped. The tink, flat and tinny, died in the big room. Try again. Hold it by the top staple. That sounds better. Perhaps I can grind the sound bow. Gottlieb does that to tune a bell.

He dug into the sand for the third and his heart jolted. Was that a hole he could feel? He tore the bell out. Yes! Right through the side.

He dug frantically for the remaining three and lined them up on the workbench. One was pebbled with sand. Another had gobbets of grey slag embedded in the bronze. The last was missing most of its rim.

How did that happen? I was careful. I followed every direction. He closed his eyes to block out the crooked rim of the bell and saw another ruined bell, another apprentice, Ben something. Heard Gottlieb shouting, Get out of my shop! You will never a founder make. Do not come back! And Gottlieb had torn Ben's indenture papers across and across and across before throwing them out the door after the retreating figure.

Cold sweat prickled along Liam's forehead. I'll hide them! I'll say I decided not to do it. No, he was here when I started. He stared, nauseated. Maybe I could...

"Gott im Himmel! What is this?"

The man looming over Liam seemed all teeth and bristling black eyebrows. A large hand swept Liam away from the workbench so violently that he staggered against the casting flasks. Flinching from their sharp corners, he backed still farther as the master founder snatched up the rimless bell and shook it under his nose. "And this is the great pour you begged

3

for? This blistered mess? This that has been nibbled by rats?"

Liam swallowed. He always felt sick when Gottlieb shouted.

"Well?" the founder prompted.

"I...I did it just as you showed me. I don't know what happened. I..." Liam choked on the words as a great hand seized him by the shoulder and hauled him towards the workbench.

"Come and learn! For this," Gottlieb picked up the rimless bell, "you did not pour smoothly."

"But I did. I..."

"I have told you. To hesitate even for a second is to spoil the pour. And for this you did not skim the slag properly."

"I'm sure I..."

"For this," the rising voice drowned out his plaintive bleat, "you did not ram the sand down firmly. And this..." He pointed to tiny holes perforating another bell. "How shall such a bell sing sweetly? That you, a so-called musician, should make such a bell!"

"I did my best," Liam muttered. And don't sneer at me, he thought, I *am* a musician. In the pockets of his leather apron, his sweaty hands clenched into fists.

"Your best?" The bellow made Liam wince. "This is your best?" The founder snatched up the perforated bell and squeezed it between his great hands until the sides collapsed. "Here is what your best deserves." He hurled the crushed bell into the scrap bin and with one sweep of his arm sent all the rest tumbling after it. "That I should have such a one for an apprentice! *Dummkopf!* Good-for-nothing Irish!"

"It was only my first time!" Liam heard himself shouting. "What do you expect?"

"Expect!" Gottlieb roared. "Have I not taught you perfectly? Should I not expect perfect results? And what do I get?" He booted the wooden flask on the floor between them. "Bells that will not ring. Bells that must be scrapped. Carelessness and wastefulness from an apprentice that I — Gottlieb Hahn — have trained." With each word his voice rose until Liam cringed from the sound, his hands over his ears. Suddenly Gottlieb lunged at the wooden flask full of sand. With a mighty effort he hoisted it above his head, then hurled it crashing to the floor. "That is what I think of your best," he roared. "Clean it up. Clean it up and start again!" And he strode out of the casting shed.

Liam sagged against the wall. "The devil take your bloody bells and..." Not even enough strength to curse, he thought, squeezing his eyes shut to stop the stinging. Was it tears or just the dust and fumes of the foundry? "I hate it here. I hate it here. I hate it here," he intoned bleakly.

"I'm so sorry, Liam. Papa shouldn't have…"

His eyes snapped open. He lurched away from the wall. How long had she been in the doorway? What had she heard? He knew from her wide-eyed stare she could see the tears. "Shut up, Rebecca," he spat. "Just shut up and leave me alone."

She fled and he dashed the tears from his eyes, leaving a sticky trail of dust and salt. Damn. Blast and damn! This hellish place. No matter what I do, it's always, Vhy you did not do this? Vhy you did not do that? He mimicked Gottlieb's Germanic speech bitterly.

He clenched his teeth to stop his chin from trembling. If only I could face up to him. If only he didn't shout all the time. I can't stand it, Da, I can't stand it any more. I know what you said. He closed his eyes, seeing again the slight figure of his father drooping in the chair as he signed the papers with almost the last of his strength. "I've made a good bargain for you," he'd said. "You'll have training. A craft. That means something in this new country." And when Liam had protested, said he wanted to go on with school, maybe even to a university, his father had smiled wanly. "And even if we had the money, Liam, what good did that do *me*? You'll have my books to feed your soul but you must have skilled hands to put bread in your mouth."

Liam inspected the hands that had let him down — fine-boned, long-fingered like his father's. With one jagged, grimy nail, he scratched at a half-healed burn itching under its scab. What musician could use these hands — or what founder either? He glanced around the cavernous room with its monster furnace. Hellish place! Fit for no one but a brutish ox like... He remembered the first time his father had suggested being a founder. " 'Tis a sound craft," his father had said. "A good skill for a growing country like Canada." But Liam hadn't thought about the future. All he could picture were the bells in Gottlieb's shop. Once, years ago, he and Rebecca had lined them up — first a tiny goat's bell, then some cow bells, a dinner bell, even one of the great locomotive bells. They'd spent a whole afternoon ringing tunes with the mallet. He'd fallen in love with bells that day. So, making them? Not a bad idea. He had to do something.

Not a bad idea? Disaster, that's what it was!

Dirt and noise and heat and sweat and smells — and no beautiful bells of his own. He looked at the scrap box and tears threatened again. What am I going to do, Da? He doesn't want me here, you know. Just because you were friends, he took me. But seven years! How can I stand it? Why ever did you sign those papers? 'Tis your fault! I never asked to be apprenticed. Maybe I'll just leave. What do you think of that, then, Da?

The idea made him feel better. What's to stop me? I could join the army. Isaac did. He remembered the furor when Gottlieb's only son had insisted on joining up. Not that Gottlieb will care what happens to me. But it would be exciting. And they were desperate for men, with the whole of Canada West in a panic over this trouble boiling up on the American border.

So how will I do it? Lie about my age and... He paused in the act of tearing off his leather apron. His age. Would they believe he was old enough? Forget it, he told himself tiredly. 'Tis no use. I'm trapped here. Not a living soul in the whole of North America cares tuppence about me. Apprenticed for seven years. Shift that sand. Haul that wood. Fetch that bucket. Sweep that floor. Bullied and shouted at the whole time. Why did you do this to me, Da?

To keep himself from thinking, he grabbed the shovel and attacked the pile of fine sand spilling out of his broken mould. He scooped and flung towards the bin, not caring that the sand puffed clouds, filling his mouth with grit. The rhythmic swinging of his arms made his pulse beat in his head, blotting out unhappy thoughts. Harder and faster he threw the sand.

Suddenly the door flew open and Gottlieb appeared. "Vhy all this dust?" he demanded, flailing at it with a roll of paper. Hard on his heels came Mr. Hansen, their next-door neighbour. He nodded at Liam as he followed the founder to the workbench by the windows. Gottlieb had unrolled the large sheet of paper and was pinning the corners with metal shears and punches.

Casually Liam sidled closer, reaching to hang up the shovel so that he could peer around Gottlieb's shoulder. He saw a drawing of a large bell, cross-sections and front views all neatly labelled with measurements. Gottlieb looked up, frowning.

"Enough, enough," he snapped. "*Raus!* Go! Tomorrow will we start again."

Liam blinked. Go! A whole two hours before supper! He snatched off his leather apron as the two men hunched back over the drawings.

This is too good to be true, he thought as he grabbed his jacket off a peg.

Just outside the door was a washstand and basin. Liam dipped icy water from the bucket and splashed it on his face, feeling the shiver go right through him. He ran wet hands through his thick red hair to plaster it down, then peered into the square of polished metal nailed to the wall. His eyes, a washed-out blue at the best of times, looked puffy. Would anyone be able to tell? What if Rebecca were in there blabbing to her aunt this very minute? Can't go in yet, he thought regretfully, wanting the warmth of the stove — tea cakes perhaps, dripping with butter. How long before his face would look normal again?

He shrugged into his jacket, hugging its warmth against the chilly March afternoon. Two hours. What can I do? Read. Where? The bell tower? He glanced at the stairs that ran up the outside of the foundry, past the charging gallery above the furnace to the roof where Gottlieb had built a cupola to hang a large bell. Years ago, Gottlieb's son, Isaac, had shown Liam what a wonderful lookout it made. If only he hadn't gone off to the army, Liam thought and felt pressure behind his eyes again.

To shake his mind free of regrets, he stamped

up the stairs and pushed open the trapdoor. The bell, a beautiful green-tinged bronze, filled most of the space. As he slithered into one of the triangles formed by the edges of the tower, Liam ran a fingernail around the curving edge, listening to the way the bell whispered and hummed. He reached up and patted its shoulder, wanting to hug it, to lay his cheek against its smooth side. Don't be stupid! he told himself.

The view, stretching farther than he could clearly see, always filled him with a sense of peace. Brown fields, splotched with the last of the snow, spread like a skirt around the foundry. He fished under the sill for the fine leather case that held his father's brass spyglass. Squinting through the eyepiece, he swung the glass and followed the dark slash of the canal south towards Lake Erie, hoping to see the army camp. On a good day, he could make out the rows of white dots that were tents in the fields skirting the lake shore. He twisted the eyepiece. No luck. Too late in the day, he decided with a sigh. I wish I were there with Isaac — any place but here! If only... Oh, what's the use?

He swung the spyglass further left — an empty road unwinding through miles of fields.

And at the end of the road…Fort Erie. Now there's a place, he thought. Remember, Da? That time we stood on the dock? The steamer unloading…come up the Erie Canal all the way from New York, it had. And those boys throwing the ropes over the bollards? I could do that. I could do that! His heart skipped a beat. In an hour I could be miles along the road. I might be in Fort Erie before they missed me. Hop a boat. They're always looking for help. What an adventure!

He looked at the greying sky. It would be dark before I was halfway there…and, anyway, heavy shipping doesn't start 'til next month. Might not find a boat. A phrase, half remembered from Latin lessons, drifted into his mind, *Carpe diem*. He heard his father's voice, "*Carpe diem* — seize the day, Liam. Put no trust in the morrow."

He shivered. Tomorrow back in the foundry? Or tomorrow somewhere else? He swung the spyglass around to look at the house where he lived with the founder and his family. The lens brought it so close that when the side door opened and Rebecca appeared, Liam flinched into the shadows. As though she could see you, he scoffed, watching as she tilted the basin and flung out the water. She lingered, staring towards the foundry. What would she say at supper? Trust Rebecca to say something. He shivered again. Too cold up here, he thought regretfully, closing the spyglass and tucking it into the pigskin bag. My legacy from you, Da, he thought, looking into the bag — a spyglass, a flute and four books. He ran a gentle finger along a satin leather binding. Latin poets, that one was. Haven't read much lately. Sorry, Da.

Two hours. A shame to waste free time. Another phrase slipped into his mind, *Vita brevis, occasio fugax*. The last thing they'd translated together. Life is short, opportunity fleeting. Opportunity. How often did he have two hours free? And he saw again the dock at Fort Erie, the lake boats... Just then the door to the foundry banged. Liam leaned over and saw far below the tiny figure of Mr. Hansen heading back to the road.

Opportunity *is* fleeting, Liam told himself. Almost without being aware, he fastened the buckles on his father's satchel and slung it by the strap over his back. All he cherished was in that bag, but in his room he had a change of clothes and two shillings. I'll need them, he thought, as he ran lightly down the stairs to the yard.

Where is everyone? He glanced at the house.

Rebecca and Aunt Thirza would be in the kitchen starting supper. He sprinted up the path, his mind bubbling with thoughts of adventure. He was on the veranda with his hand on the doorknob when his eye caught a flicker of movement. A corner of the parlour curtain twitched. Rebecca! He wouldn't be through the door before she'd be after him, wanting to know what he was up to. The smell of roasting meat made his mouth water. No! I'm going to do it. Try and see this, Miss Nosy, he thought, and he ducked behind the house.

Pounding down the roadway, with the shock of the hard-baked surface thudding up through his body, he could feel his frustration and confusion shaking loose. The devil take them all, he thought, putting distance between himself and the foundry. The devil take them all. I'm free!

Sweat was streaming down his face when he finally stopped. He leaned against a tree at the side of the road to catch his breath and get his bearings. How far had he come? A mile? No — more, surely. But, 'tis fourteen miles to Fort Erie and the dark coming on, he thought. A rumbling in his stomach reminded him of supper steaming on the stove. You've decided, he told himself, slinging the leather wallet over his shoulder — so get on with it!

The road before him was deserted. Good! No neighbours to report seeing him. And none of the strangers seen around lately, either. Rough customers, Gottlieb had called them and warned his family to keep in at nights. Of course, who knows what's around the bend? Liam thought as he started off again at a brisk trot. He tried not to think what dangers might be ahead but he couldn't stop the voice nagging at him. "Now why would you be doing this, Liam?" His father's voice, reasonable, reasoning. "It looks for all the world like cutting off your nose to spite your face. Just be thinking awhile."

"I'm not listening." Liam all but shouted. "You got me into this. What made you think I could be a founder? Why did you have to die?" How many times had he asked his father those questions this last year?

Ah, forget all that, he told himself. There's an adventure at the end of this road. Chin jutting, he marched on. The rhythmic tramp started a tune in his head — or *was* it in his head? He seemed to hear a distant whistling. The melody, lilting and mournful, was vaguely familiar. As he listened, the music drew closer and with it the sound of footsteps clipping along the hard-packed surface of the road. Instinctively Liam quickened his pace, glancing apprehensively behind him. An unfamiliar figure was rapidly overtaking him. As he came within hailing distance, the man raised a hand in greeting.

"Well met, cousin!"

CHAPTER

TWO

"A good even' t'you, Liam."

Liam spun around. A slender young man stood before him, not a head taller than himself. I know that face. How do I know that face? And hair like that... He stared at the black hair curling from beneath the turned-up brim. Then the stranger smiled, a three-cornered smile that lifted his cheeks and crinkled the skin around his eyes. Aunt Kate, Liam thought. No. It's impossible! But his heart was beating wildly as he extended his hand and felt it grasped and wrung.

"Well, cousin, 'tis a long search I've made to find you and that's no word of a lie."

Liam felt his mouth sagging open and snapped it shut. "Cousin? You did say 'cousin'?"

"I did that. Do you not recognize this face, then?" He leaned closer and Liam had to step back to focus clearly. "I'm said to have a great look of me mam about me. And wasn't it herself held your own dear mother in her arms as she died, God rest her soul?"

Tears pricked behind Liam's eyes. He saw his five-year-old self peering over the end of the bed, heard his mother moaning as his Aunt Kate propped her up and held a cup to her lips, felt himself taken by the shoulders and hustled from the room. "You're Aunt Kate's son?" he croaked.

"Aye, I am that, me boy. Patrick Danaghy himself, your most obedient servant." He swept off his hat and flourished it in Liam's direction. "Now, will you be joining me on this rail?" The stranger beckoned towards the wooden fence that snaked beside the road. "I could do with sitting down for a spell." He shrugged a small pack off his back, tossed it by the fence post and swung himself onto the top rail.

Liam just stood and stared. So many things about this man tugged at his memory and yet… "Patrick ran off to America."

"True as you say it, cousin. Indeed I did. And

18

an interesting time I've had of it, ever since." He hooked the toes of shabby boots under the lower rail, then hunched into a comfortable perch. "Will you not join me up here? 'Tis sorry I am to have nothing better to offer me own blood cousin than a fence, but the times are strange. We must all make do with what's to hand and that's God's own truth."

"Do you mean to say you've been searching for me?" Liam demanded. He heard the urgency in his own voice and was surprised at how much he wanted the answer.

"Indeed I have. And a long search it's been, too. You might have dropped right off the face of the earth for all anyone knew a thing about you from the time your da winkled you out of me mother's arms to this very minute."

Liam frowned. "We wrote back. We wrote as often as we could afford to." He searched Patrick's face and was alarmed to see a closed and secretive look. Then the smile flashed sure and strong and Liam relaxed again.

"Indeed I've not a doubt of it." The voice was soft and caressing. "And haven't I been away myself, a stranger in a strange land? Four years in the Union Army. Never the same place to lay me head twice in a week and me letters from home trailing me all over the countryside. But one day I says to myself, there's Liam, me own mother's sister's child, another stranger in a strange land. Bedad, I'll find him. So I slung me pack on me back and started out."

He smiled and Liam felt dizzy with excitement.

"Many a long weary mile have I travelled looking for you, me boy. But here I am and here you are — at last," the hypnotic voice continued. "And what could be nicer than sitting with me own cousin? And him with a face that none could mistake for anything but a loyal Irishman true born."

The soft, lilting sentences spun a web of delight around Liam and he was once more in his aunt's white stone cottage with the smell of the peat fire in his nostrils and the taste of buttered scones on his tongue. Suddenly he realized that Patrick was gazing at him intently.

"Did you ask me something, cousin?" He liked the sound of that word "cousin." "You brought Ireland back so strongly I was off in a daydream."

"And is that not just as it should be? We none of us should forget our own true home, me boy."

Yes, Liam thought, that's what I'm missing.

That's what makes the difference. Belonging. Being kin. "But how did you find me?"

Patrick hesitated, then shrugged. "A lot of looking and a little luck. What's it matter now it's done? But enough of me own chatter. What about you? How came you here?"

"Well…" Liam searched his mind for a place to start. "When my father came to fetch me, we had to escape at night, wade out to a boat offshore." He saw again his younger self riding on his father's shoulders out to a fishing smack. Remembering the danger, the fear of pursuit, made his pulse race. "Of course, once we were in England there was no danger, but my father decided Canada was a better place for us. He was offered a job in Stonebridge — schoolmaster. So we fetched up here five years ago and…" He glanced up. "Did you know my father had died?"

"Aye. And sorry I was to hear it. Would ye be telling me just a little of how it happened?"

"Consumption," Liam said bleakly. "He had a weak chest. From that bullet he took in the lungs. When he and your father had to escape."

"*My* father didn't escape." The soft voice grew suddenly harsh.

Liam swallowed and looked away, his stomach churning. What does he expect? I was only

21

a year old when it all happened. And another eight years before I set eyes on my own father. But part of him felt ashamed. After all, his aunts had told him the story all his life. The student riot in Dublin. The magistrate clubbed to death. His father and uncle on the run. His father escaping from Ireland but Patrick's father, another Liam, caught and hanged.

"Ah well, be blowed to that for old history." Patrick waved his hand as though to erase the memory, and the lilt was back in his voice. "Tell me what's become of you ever since."

Relieved, Liam plunged in. "When he knew he was dying, he apprenticed me so I'd have a craft and be able to keep myself. At Hahn's Foundry, down the road to Stonebridge, there, just before the canal."

"Ah, yes. I know the place. And would they be treating you well?"

Liam turned to pour out all the hurt and anger. He'll understand. Just like Da would. He took a breath, then remembered, Patrick's been a soldier. What if he thinks me a cry-baby? He clamped his teeth on the complaints. "Well enough," he said, tightly.

"Good. Delighted I am to hear it." Something in his tone made Liam scan the triangular face. The eyes were half-closed making his cousin look, for a moment, almost sly. Your imagination's working overtime, Liam told himself, as the odd pointed smile turned up all the corners of Patrick's face and Liam could see again the face of his Aunt Kate, of his mother. They were a green-eyed, black-haired people, his mother's family. Liam looked more like his father — blue eyes, rusty-red hair and a thousand freckles. Potato Irish, he'd heard a neighbour sniff to Rebecca's aunt one day. He preferred the black and green colouring of his mother's family. Patrick's green eyes were flecked with yellow — cat's eyes, Liam thought.

"Now tell me, cousin…" The soft voice broke into his musings. "How would you be feeling about a bit of an adventure?"

Liam sat up so straight that he nearly over-balanced. "How did you know?" he stuttered.

"Know what, me boy?"

"Why, that I'm…" The words were hard to get out. "I'm running away." There. That made it real. And then everything came tumbling out. "I've had enough of Mr. Gottlieb Hahn and his stinking foundry. It's Fort Erie and a ship for me. Look, there's my kit." He pointed to the leather bag he'd dropped beside the fence. A refrain was running through his head. It was meant. It was meant. Running away from that drudgery. Off to find adventure, and it comes walking up to meet me. I was meant to meet Patrick. Whatever the adventure, I'm ready. I'll take the chance.

"Ah, running away, is it? But you did say they treated you well in that place down the road."

"I didn't say 'well'. I said 'well enough'." Now he thinks I'm making it up, Liam berated himself.

"So you're ripe for an adventure then, are you?"

"Yes, yes!" Liam stammered. "Wherever you're going, I'll come with you. I'll do whatever you want," he finished fervently.

"With never a hint of what it's all about?"

Was that mockery he heard in the light voice? Well, let him laugh. Liam lifted his chin and stared Patrick in the eye. "Yes," he said again.

"Now there's spirit for you. But you see, it's not quite a question of coming with me."

"But…What, then?" Liam felt the exhilaration dying.

"That foundry down the road. You've the run of it, do you?"

"Of course. I'm the apprentice." Impatience made his tone sharp.

"Ever been up the top? In that bell tower?"

"Yes. Certainly." Where was this leading?

Was there to be an adventure or not?

"And I've never a doubt from there you can see all the goings on around and about?"

"And why would you want to know that?" The feeling of sick disappointment flooding through Liam made the question sound truculent, sullen.

But Patrick just cocked his head to the side and smiled slightly. "Well now, cousin," he said, "there's a little something about to happen and it would be very helpful to certain people to know a bit of what was going on about the countryside."

Liam felt as though a great rock had thumped him on the chest. Of course. He should have known. "You're a Fenian!" he blurted out.

The yellow-green eyes turned hard as agate. Liam couldn't breathe under that searching gaze. Then Patrick was smiling again. "I am indeed a member of that illustrious brotherhood — as were my father and your father before us. 'Tis in their blessed memory I've come seeking you, Liam O'Brien."

"Me? Me!"

"Yes, you, cousin — if you indeed have the heart to undertake a great adventure."

"But I've told you…"

"Ah, but you want to be off travelling. What

25

I'm asking takes more courage than that."

More courage than setting off into the unknown? But—"What would you want me to do?"

"I can't tell you that, cousin, until I know you're the man for the job."

"But if I'm not to come with you... How can I prove...?"

"By doing exactly what I ask of you. Go back to the foundry and wait."

"No." Liam set his chin. "I've made up my mind. I..."

Patrick checked him with a raised hand. "Then you're not the man I'm after." The voice was heavy. Was that disappointment Liam could hear? His cousin's shoulders sagged. He slid slowly off the top rail, sighing as he landed on the ground. For a moment he leaned against the fence.

"Wait. Wait! I didn't mean... It's just that..." Liam stumbled over his words, frantically searching his mind as his cousin swung his pack over his shoulder and settled it on his back. Then he looked straight at Liam, a faint, sad smile on his face. What have I done? Liam thought. My only kin this side of the water and I can't even listen to what he wants.

"It's not that I'm set on travelling," he started.

"It's just that…" What was so bad about the foundry? It all seemed such an age ago. He could hardly remember the emotions that had sent him off down the road. And to have Patrick walk out of his life forever… "Tell me what you want," he heard himself saying, "and I'll do it."

The smile widened and Liam felt warm and comforted. Patrick's arm came around his shoulders. "Now there's a man for you. Didn't I know the minute I set eyes on you, you'd a lion's heart in you?" The arm tightened around Liam, then dropped. "Now, here's me plan," he continued briskly. "I must be off and away for a few days, but one week from tonight I'll be back. An hour before sunset, on this very spot. If I find you waiting for me, then I'll know you're truly my man. How's that for a bargain, cousin?"

Liam hesitated. If only… Yes. No. Can? Can't? I must know just a little more. He took a deep breath. "This has something to do with the Fenians across the river at Buffalo, doesn't it?" He stared hard at his cousin, willing him to speak. Patrick's face was bland, unreadable.

"Now isn't that a dark night coming up the road," was all he said. "And us needing to be on our way. Walk with me to the crossroads yonder. Our paths divide there — for the present."

As he spoke he linked arms with Liam.

"No, wait." Liam grabbed up his leather bag as Patrick urged them towards the roadway. "You must tell me... I don't understand..." he stammered.

"Liam, Liam, 'tis many a long talk we must have before you'll understand all there is to know. You must trust me. Until next week, cousin..."

"Just tell me one thing... St. Patrick's Day... the Fenians were supposed to invade... we heard all sorts of rumours..."

"Now when can you ever believe a rumour, young Liam? Never you worry. Nothing exciting will happen before I get back to tell you about it. And another thing—" Patrick had stopped walking. He took Liam's face between his hands and stared so intently that Liam could scarcely keep from blinking. "With the times as they are no one must know you've an Irish cousin roaming the peninsula. So, never a word to a living soul. Swear."

"I swear."

"On your mother's grave."

"I swear on my mother's grave." Liam's heart was pounding again. The hard eyes seemed to probe to the bottom of his soul.

"And isn't that a fine cousin for a man to

have?" Patrick cried, clapping Liam on the shoulder. "Remember, one week from tonight!" Then he turned on his heel and was striding off down the road, filling the air with the mournful whistling that had announced his arrival.

CHAPTER

THREE

Liam shivered and sneezed. Should move, he thought.

Instead he stood puzzling over the past half hour. His cousin. His very own cousin. And a Fenian to boot! He felt a glow of pride. He didn't know much about the Fenians, but they were Irish and they seemed to want the same sort of things his father had wanted — a free Ireland. He'd never quite been able to figure out what they were doing over here in North America but still, he'd been a little hurt when Isaac had been so keen to join the army. "It's not Irish I'm fighting," Isaac had insisted, "it's invaders." Others weren't so particular, Liam reflected wryly, remembering dirty looks flung at him in town after all the trouble blew up. Not just him, of course — anyone with a touch of Irish on his tongue.

Still, what exactly did Patrick want with him? To go back to the foundry and wait! For what? If he'd never come, Liam thought, I'd be halfway to Fort Erie by now. He looked down the dark road and swallowed. The grumble in his stomach had become a hard, insistent pain.

What will I do? Think. Think! If I go back... Do what Patrick wants... Wait and find out what will happen...? And after all, Patrick is family, blood of my blood... What if, Liam thought, catching his breath at a new and startling thought, what if Patrick is a sending from my father? What if some sort of fate meant me to be apprenticed here? And the difficulties with Gottlieb? A test to see if I'm worthy. And, after all, Patrick is kin. Someone who belongs to me by right of birth.

Make up your mind. The sky had gone nearly black. He could barely see his own length down the road. And Aunt Thirza would have supper on the table. At the thought his mouth began to water. Had he been given a sign? Was he meant to stay? Decide. Decide! Then, almost without knowing it, he was running down the road, back towards Stonebridge.

31

He was panting and breathless when he stumbled finally into the side yard. He leaned his head against the porch upright and waited for his racing heart to slow. My bag, he thought, a place to stow it, or Rebecca might guess what I've been up to. The warm glow from the kitchen window picked out benches that ran along the wall and with a sigh of relief he slung his case beneath one, then glanced quickly through the window. Might as well see what I'm walking into, he decided.

The scene inside seemed far away, almost as though he were watching strangers through the wrong end of his spyglass. Aunt Thirza at the black iron stove stirring a huge pot of soup — brisk, that's what he always thought when he saw her swishing about the house. But kind enough. He had no quarrel with Aunt Thirza. Gottlieb in his chair beside the stove peering short-sightedly at the newspaper. Somehow, in the kitchen, he didn't seem as big, as frightening as he did in the foundry. Rebecca, clattering soup bowls onto the table, glanced up. He caught her eye through the pane of glass and the scene refocused, felt normal again.

Right, he thought, now or never. Smoothing the sweat-streaked hair out of his eyes, he opened the door and slipped in. The sudden warmth made him shiver. What if someone asks where I've been? he wondered as the latch clicked behind him. He braced himself for questions but Gottlieb didn't even glance up. Aunt Thirza met his eyes for a long steady moment. She said nothing, but Liam could tell from the way her eyes studied him, kind and worried, that Rebecca had told her all about the set-to in the foundry. He turned to glare at Rebecca rattling knives and spoons onto the big kitchen table. How dare she interfere! Did she think he needed to hide behind her aunt's apron?

Rebecca threw him a sideways glance, then whisked over to reach behind him for the plates stacked ready on the counter of the dish cupboard. "I saw you sneaking off," she murmured too softly for the adults to hear. "Where did you go?"

"Why should I be telling you?" he snapped and had the satisfaction of seeing anger redden her cheeks.

"Supper, all," Aunt Thirza announced. "Rebecca, put those plates on the table and fetch the potatoes and onions out of the warming oven. Quickly now!"

As he stood behind his chair waiting for Gottlieb and Aunt Thirza, Liam let irritation sweep through him. Why did she have to be so nosy? Always wanting to know everything about a person. Right from the first time they met. The day his father was appointed schoolmaster of the local middle school that was, and Gottlieb, as chairman of the school trustees, had invited them to Sunday dinner. The adults had gone inside, leaving the two nine-year-olds out on the porch. He remembered shifting from foot to foot, tongue-tied because he wasn't used to girls. "Lee-yum?" she said. "I thought your name was William."

"So it is. Liam for short."

"For short, for sure." She looked down from her extra three inches. "I think I'll call you Willie. Wee Willie, that's you."

Incensed, he caught hold of her long black braid. "How would you like a bath in the canal?"

"From you and who else?" she laughed. Twitching the braid from his grasp, she flounced off. It hadn't taken Rebecca three seconds to realize he wasn't about to push a girl into the canal. Not a great beginning, but they'd become pretty good friends, roaming through fields and streams hunting rabbits and weasels and frogs. Maybe because we had something in common, Liam decided, he newly arrived and feeling strange, Rebecca with her mother just dead and an aunt she scarcely knew in charge of the household.

Chair legs scraped. Liam slid into his seat opposite Rebecca. Gottlieb asked the blessing — too long as usual, Liam grumbled to himself as his stomach protested each second's delay, but eventually soup was steaming in his bowl and he forgot everything but food.

Two helpings later, in mid-reach for another slice of bread, he caught Rebecca watching him. He'd seen that speculative look on her face before. May the devil swallow me sideways, Liam vowed to himself, before you get one word about Patrick out of me, Rebecca Hahn.

"Clear the plates, please, children," Aunt Thirza said and then turned to her brother. "Well, Gottlieb, tell us what is going on out in the world. What are the newspapers saying about these Fenians?"

Liam's hand jerked and his fork clattered to his plate. "Sorry," he muttered as all the heads swivelled. Watch it! he told himself. What if they suspect…? Suspect what? Nothing's happened — yet. But for once, he found himself listening carefully as Gottlieb grumbled about the week's news.

"Ach, Fenians! They will not come."

"How can you say that when the papers have been…"

"Ach, Thirza! The papers. What do they know?"

"Didn't John Macdonald himself call out the militia?"

"Ach, politicians. Three months has that army been training and of invaders have we seen not a hair. A waste of time. Worse! A waste of money. This we will not discuss."

Good, Liam thought. I can do without talk of Fenians. He pushed his chair back and lifted the empty plate from Aunt Thirza's place. Patrick had called it a "great and glorious brotherhood"—the very words his father once used about the Young Irelanders. Were Fenians the same? And what about that pedlar last month who said the Fenians were part of a plot by the American government to invade Canada? If only I knew for sure…

Lost in thought, he carried the dishes to the pantry where Rebecca was stacking soup bowls for washing.

"Well?" she said. "Where did you go this afternoon?"

Damn! He'd forgotten she'd be at him the

minute she got him alone. "Mind your own business…" he started, then turned to listen as he realized what Aunt Thirza was saying.

"…a stranger," she finished.

"When do we not have strangers? The canal brings many such."

"Yes, but they pass on through. This one's been lurking about…"

"I know who you mean!" Rebecca dashed back to the table. "I saw him again today. A bit older than Isaac. He wears an army hat. You know those big brimmed ones. And…"

Liam's heart jolted. That hat Patrick wore — it was an American army hat. But … lurking about? No. Patrick had only just arrived. Hadn't he?

"He's certainly been around this past week," Aunt Thirza agreed. "Just walking along the road or down by the canal. Now if that's not spying…"

"Imagine," Rebecca breathed as Liam sat down slowly. "A Fenian spy on our very doorstep!"

"Enough. *Ruhig!*" Gottlieb put down his teacup and looked around his table. "Speculation will nothing but panic achieve."

"Nevertheless…" His sister's tone was equally determined. Liam liked to hear her get the better of Gottlieb. "Nevertheless we must be on the alert for danger. We are too close to the canal and the railway line to take chances."

"Cautious, yes," her brother agreed, "but not, like some of our good neighbours, hysterical. What do we know of these so-called Fenians? A group of men camps on the other side of the Niagara River. Rumour says they are soldiers who will invade. For three months they do nothing. So! There is no call for panic, strangers or no strangers."

Liam, looking from brother to sister, caught Rebecca doing the same. They exchanged questioning glances. Who would win? Thirza's mouth tightened, but all she said was, "Rebecca, bring in the pie." This round to Gottlieb.

When the kitchen was tidy and they were all sitting at a comfortable distance around the iron stove, Gottlieb said, "A little music please, Rebecca."

"Papa, it's chilly in the parlour. I can't play when my hands are cold."

"Make up the fire, then. And Liam will read to us from the newspaper while you do that."

Liam looked up from the paper. Oh, will I, he thought with a stab of resentment. Orders, orders, that's all I get around here. He ran his finger down the columns looking for interesting tidbits. You expect us all to dance to your tune, don't you. Well, just you wait...

"First the editorial," Gottlieb directed and Liam's roving finger found the black-bordered square. Fenians! it screamed and Liam felt his stomach flip. Not again. Not now. Just then Rebecca came flying out of the parlour and settled herself across the table with her embroidery. They all looked expectantly at him. His throat felt scratchy and hoarse. Sure, it was his turn to read, but it was supposed to be the next chapter of *Great Expectations*.

"No attempt has been made..." He coughed again to clear his throat. "No attempt has been made by the Fenians to invade Canada." Well, we know that! "Although reported to be drilling in the Buffalo area, these demented creatures..." Rebecca giggled. Liam glared at her. Idiot! "...these demented creatures did not launch the expected attack against the sovereign rights of the Queen and the security of her subjects. Even though the alarm has somewhat subsided, there has been no abatement in the defensive preparations."

"No abatement, indeed!" Gottlieb snorted. "Wasting the time of honest workmen. Teaching idleness and frivolity to young men."

"The governor general has stated," Liam

continued, "that the ten thousand volunteers now in the militia will be maintained under arms for the present to provide protection for the lives and property of Canadians against the threatened piratical attacks of men who use the territory of a neighbouring power openly to organize these lawless enterprises."

Liam paused, expecting some comment. He glanced at Gottlieb, who merely gestured to him to continue. "The Fenians' avowed motives include revenge upon England for Ireland's alleged wrongs. They propose to assail Canada as a means of insult and annoyance more within their reach and more easily compassed than England herself."

"There," Gottlieb broke in. "That is what this nonsense is all about. An insult, an annoyance. Like children they are squabbling and the rest of us must suffer for it."

Liam felt himself go hot all over. How dare he pass judgement when he knew nothing. "They do have reason!" Three pairs of eyes turned on him. My God, had he said that out loud? His father's words poured through his mind. As though from a great distance he heard himself say, "English oppression for two hundred years. Children not allowed to go to school. Growing up ignorant. Unfit to work.

And then the famine. People starving when the potatoes rotted in the fields. And the English government did nothing." He felt himself choking. Don't cry. Whatever happens, don't cry!

"And when you were in Ireland you were not taught to read and write?" Gottlieb's voice, flat and passionless.

"Well, yes, I…"

"And when you were in Ireland you went hungry every night to bed?"

"No." He could feel his face going red. Damn Gottlieb. Always trying to put him in the wrong.

"Ach, so!"

"But that was because…"

"Read on," Gottlieb commanded.

And if I refuse? Liam gritted his teeth, saw Aunt Thirza furrowing her brow as she glanced from master to apprentice, and thought, Who cares? I might not be here after next week. He took a deep breath and read on.

"The Canadian Catholic Bishop Lynch has issued a circular denouncing Fenianism and calling upon the people to repel the invasion. The president of the St. Patrick's Society in Montreal has vowed that all Irishmen will back their loyalty with their strong right arms."

"There! That is what sensible men think of these Fenians."

Smug, self-satisfied, bullying... Liam choked on the words he was biting back. What did Gottlieb know about Irish suffering? If only he could remember...argue as persuasively as his father. If only Patrick... No, don't think about Patrick... might give something away.

"I hope you've finished with that boring stuff," Rebecca said.

Liam folded the paper with a snap, thinking, We certainly have.

"Rebecca, we were to have some music."

"Oh, Papa, I just have a few more stitches."

"'A Mighty Fortress Is Our God.' The parlour is now warm and we all need the comfort of good Master Luther to send us tranquil to bed."

As Rebecca flounced off to the parlour, Liam ran his finger along the puzzles scattered among the articles but his mind would not concentrate. The opening chords of the hymn rolled through the house, square and solid and loud. At the back of his mind, Liam heard a whisper of a different music. He hadn't thought for years about evenings in his aunt's parlour. There, a fiddler and a fifer would whirl them through jigs or croon them to sleep with lullabies. Tears stung his eyes. Why did you bring me here, Da? Patrick was right. I am a stranger in a strange land.

He pictured his aunts with their thin, clever faces and quick smiles. So different from square and stolid Aunt Thirza, frowning at the sock she was mending. He had been encouraged to call her "aunt" years ago when Sunday dinner with the Hahns became a fixed part of the O'Briens' schedule. She had always made him feel welcome, but this was not her house. It was Gottlieb's. And he had always been nervous of that stern, taciturn man. With his father there had been laughter even if, at the end, the laughter had been followed by violent fits of coughing. If only he hadn't died. If only...

Well, Liam sighed, wishing the past undone won't help the present. Where had he heard that? One of his aunts probably. He turned back to the newspaper. "All Irishmen will back their loyalty with their strong right arms," it said. Loyalty to whom? To what? And are the Fenians "demented creatures"? Patrick certainly didn't seem demented. And yet he had admitted to being a Fenian. Another thought struck Liam. Does it matter what I feel about any of this? I'm too young to fight on either side. And too clumsy to be of any use in the foundry.

How I'd like to show them. I'll find a way. Just wait. Looking down, he saw his fist crumpling the corner of the paper. He was furtively smoothing the creases as the last chords of the hymn came crashing out of the parlour.

CHAPTER

FOUR

All week Liam hugged to himself the thought of an adventure.

No, not just an adventure, he thought fiercely as he swept the floor of the foundry. Patrick said "a great adventure." Something important. And in two more days I'll know. Just two more days!

The time had ticked by painfully since that evening encounter. 'Tis a great life I have here to be sure in Master Bell Founder Gottlieb Hahn's fine establishment. Lugging wood, fetching water, sweeping, tidying. Maybe I did make a mess of one or two bells. But I could do the easier stuff, couldn't I? ...couldn't I? Polish, say, or help with a pour. Maybe not be in charge, but help. That's how a person learns. That's what Da always said. "Help me with this, Liam. Get the feel of it and then you'll be able to do it yourself." But oh no. Not Master Great Founder Hahn. Liam gave the side of the workbench a smack with the broom that sent shock waves up his arms to the shoulders. Get it right the first try or back to the baby stuff, the scut work for stupid old Liam. Well, not for much longer, just wait 'til Patrick's back. Then there'll be something real to do. Something important.

Yes, but what? Strange, this whole business of Fenians camped across the Niagara. For months, years maybe, he'd heard people talking nervously about invasion. But it was the Americans they expected, not the Irish! The papers always seemed full of Yankee threats to turn the "northern colonies" into American states. But this? Ach, well... Patrick will explain. Two more days!

He brushed the pile of dust and sand over to the open door, then glanced around. Good. No one looking out the windows of the house. With a quick flip of the broom, he sent the dust puffing over the doorsill. That'll do for today. He smiled grimly as he remembered one of Gottlieb's favourite sayings: "Sufficient unto the day is the evil thereof." Sufficient indeed, Liam thought, giving a last swipe with the broom. "Tidy up," Gottlieb had said as he went off to make his deliveries, "and mind you do it well." He expected the sweepings to be deposited neatly in the dustbin but... Whistling, Liam closed the door and tossed the broom, javelin-like, into the corner. Now for the flasks. He started to stack the wooden frames used for yesterday's castings, then paused. What was that tune? He whistled louder trying to remember the words. Something about "water" and "daughter." Then, he had it. Eyes closed, he murmured,

> Silent, O Moyle, be the roar of thy water,
>> Break not, ye breezes, your chain of repose,
> While murmuring mournfully,
>> Lir's lonely daughter
> Tells to the night star her tale of woes.

An old Irish song. But he'd heard it recently. Yes, that tune Patrick was whistling. Strange song for a soldier, Liam thought. The children of an old Irish god, Lir, were changed into swans by their wicked stepmother and doomed to fly for nine hundred years the wild and angry Straits of Moyle. Fionnuala, the eldest, protected her brothers from the ice and snow with her body. How did it end? He couldn't quite remember. But his father had never liked it. Not because it was melancholy — he had loved the sad story of the Minstrel Boy off to war with his father's sword and harp. But "not Fionnuala," he'd always say. Odd that Patrick should be whistling it. You'd expect something brisker from a soldier.

Oh, well, just another little mystery to ask Patrick about. He set the last flask in place, then regarded the stack. Too tall? A little unsteady? It'll do, he thought, giving it a gentle nudge so that it leaned into the corner. Now what? Fill the water barrel. Glumly Liam picked up the tin pail. Twenty-five trips to the well it took. He'd counted them once. Oh, let it wait for a minute.

He sat down on the stool and gazed up at the rafters. An adventure. Would he be going off with Patrick? Or maybe it would be like those old stories of his father's. His thoughts drifted back. He could almost feel the warmth of snuggling into the crook of his father's arm with a fire in front of them and a black winter's evening beyond the door. His father's voice, resonating through his chest where Liam had nestled his head, would boom hollowly in his ear. Stirring tales his father wove so that out of the flames of that winter fire strode long-ago Irish heroes, Cuchulain the Red or the giant Finn McCool. And some from not so long ago. The Young Irelanders riding about the country in disguise, striking blows for the downtrodden peasants against their English oppressors. If only he could have ridden at his father's side. His eyes closed, his head drooped... Hoof beats drummed through his dream. He felt the horse beneath him pounding along the dirt road. He shortened the reins until the leather bit into his palms. They were riding flat out. Behind them came the shouts of their pursuers...

A door slammed. Liam's heart jolted. What was that? Through the window he could see Gottlieb crossing the strip of gravelled drive between the house and the foundry. The pail! He grabbed and ran. "Damn this place," he snarled. He shouldered the back door open and shot into the yard just as Gottlieb opened the front door. Why do I have to be chained here?

And then suddenly, the next afternoon, he was free. He was supposed to have an afternoon to himself every two weeks — it was written right into his apprentice papers — but with Isaac away and the work piling up, he couldn't count on it. Just as he'd be getting fed up enough to ask, Gottlieb would unexpectedly say, "Enough!" and that would be it — freedom for a precious few hours. This time the release came early, right at noon as they were finishing dinner.

As Liam pushed his chair away from the table, Gottlieb looked up. His black eyebrows snapped together and Liam's stomach flipped. What now!

"I have matters to attend to this afternoon. We will close the shop. You I will not need."

"Thank you," Liam stammered to Gottlieb's back as the founder disappeared into the parlour. Grouchy even about nice things, Liam thought. Never mind. I'll go up to the bell tower. Have a look around with the spyglass. Take my flute. Haven't practised for days... Deep in his daydream, he carried two plates towards the pantry.

Rebecca came zipping past him with more dishes. "Isn't it wonderful, Liam," she cried. "We can go into town..."

"Town! I don't want to go into town."

"Rebecca," Aunt Thirza's voice broke in. "I told you I don't want you going near that town. It was bad enough when we just had navvies rolling out of those grog shops but now there's soldiers as well."

"Oh, Aunt, they're not really soldiers. They're just volunteers — and Liam will be with me."

"Indeed and I won't, Rebecca." He plunked the dishes beside the drysink to emphasize his point. Rule number one with Rebecca, stand your ground.

"And Isaac will be there," she hurried on as though he hadn't spoken. "We should take some food. Heaven knows what he gets to eat, Aunt. He might be skin and bones before he gets back here. Shouldn't we just take him some of that shepherd's pie we made yesterday and some sausages…"

You crafty witch, Liam thought, then grinned as her aunt said sharply, "You don't fool me one whit, miss. I know very well you're not all that worried about your brother. You just want to get away down to the town." No flies on Aunt Thirza.

"Still," she continued, "I'm sure he would like some good home-cooked food. But only if Liam stays right with you, mind."

"Liam…" Rebecca turned beseeching eyes on him.

Thanks a lot, Liam groaned. Oh well, I wouldn't mind seeing Isaac. It's been weeks. And the camp might be interesting. He looked at Rebecca almost dancing with impatience. "Well…" he said slowly, folding his arms and gazing up at the ceiling. "Yeah. I guess so. Hate to see Isaac starve." No need to let her think she'd won.

"Wonderful!" She spun him around, catching him up in a dance.

"Don't," he said, shaking himself loose.

"Honestly, Liam. You're no fun any more. What's wrong with you?"

"Nothing," he muttered, backing away.

"Leave the boy alone, Rebecca. Come and help me pack these baskets." Before Rebecca turned to go, she gave Liam a speculative look that made him feel uneasy about the long walk into town. Well, she's not going to find out one thing about Patrick.

* * *

Twenty minutes later, Liam picked up the bigger of the two baskets Aunt Thirza had ready on the kitchen table. "Hurry up if you're coming," he called over his shoulder as Rebecca buttoned her long winter cloak.

He was opening the picket gate onto the roadway when she caught up with him. "Don't walk so fast, Liam," she panted as he set a steady pace down the road.

"You want to get there, don't you?"

52

"And don't be cross. You know very well you're just as eager to see the camp as I am."

"I don't mind seeing the camp," Liam admitted, "but I give you fair warning, Rebecca Hahn, if you ask me one nosy question, I'll turn right around and go home again. And then where will you be?"

"I wasn't going to ask you any nosy questions. I just wanted to know…"

"I'm warning you! And what's more…" He suddenly felt it was time to tell Rebecca a thing or two. A person liked some privacy, after all. When Da was alive, when there'd just been the two of them, he could read or play the flute or just stare into space if it suited him. Now, every time he turned around somebody was nattering at him.

"All right, Liam," Rebecca snapped, interrupting his thoughts. "We'll just walk along like perfect strangers."

"Don't be so silly." She always took things the wrong way.

They walked in frosty silence until the basket bumping against his knee started a tune in his mind and he found himself whistling it out loud. Rebecca joined in with the words and as he switched into harmony, he felt the lump of anger under his breastbone dissolve. It's the music, he thought. There hasn't been enough music since Da died.

"Another," suggested Rebecca and Liam, without meaning to, started into "Fionnuala's Song." His high tenor, trained by his father, soared effortlessly over the mournful intervals.

When shall the swan, her death-note singing
   Sleep, with wings in darkness furled?
When will heav'n, its sweet bell ringing,
   Call my spirit from this stormy world?

"How sad. I've never heard you sing that before. Where did you learn it?"

Liam shrugged. "Just remembered it. Come on. The bridge is free." He hurried on to divert her attention.

All foot traffic and wagons had to funnel over the swing bridge to reach the two villages that sprawled along the west side of the canal. "Quick! There's a wagon coming." He pointed to a huge delivery wagon piled high with barrels. It could hold them up for ten minutes if it lumbered onto the narrow bridge before they were across.

He caught Rebecca's arm and they dashed across the bridge just before the wagon blocked their way. Liam was pulling Rebecca towards the main street when she shook him off. "Look — some of the volunteers," and she pointed down the road. Marching towards them came a squad of young men, their tunics sombre against the greys and browns of the winter landscape. At the bridge, the sergeant in charge halted them in a ragged stamping of heavy leather boots.

"Straighten that line," he bellowed. "Steady! Forwar-r-r-d MARCH! Right wheel." And the squad swung onto the tow-path that ran along-side the canal.

"Isaac! Isaac!"

At the end of the line a head swivelled and then snapped forward again.

"For goodness' sake, Rebecca, he's on duty. Do you want to get him court-martialled?"

"Court-martialled? For saying hello to his sister?"

"Don't you know anything?"

"He's only a volunteer!"

"He's wearing a uniform. I don't suppose they give uniforms to people so they can stop whatever they're doing and have a chat. D'ye not see that sergeant? A face like a bulldog! He'd probably chew Isaac's arm off as soon as look at him."

Rebecca started to laugh. "I'd forgotten how funny you can be, Liam. You've been such a grouch lately."

The answering grin faded from Liam's face. "Yes, well..." he muttered and turned away to pick up the basket he'd set down while the squad passed.

"There! Things like that never used to make you cross."

"Will you just come along? We've another mile to go and this basket's heavy."

Liam started towards the street that ran parallel to the canal and the tow-path, setting a good pace to keep Rebecca from dawdling by the store windows. He liked looking in them himself, especially the ship chandler's where he often spent hours on his afternoon off. But not today, he thought, or we'll never get there and back before dark.

On the outskirts of the village were the grog shops Aunt Thirza had so deplored but at this time of year, with no ships on the canal, they were quiet. Even so, Liam felt an obligation to hurry Rebecca past them.

He walked fast, striding out even though he could hear Rebecca puffing beside him. He wanted quiet to think. That unexpected glimpse of Isaac had left him feeling all churned up inside. He hadn't really thought through what Isaac was doing out here. He liked working alongside Isaac in the foundry… learning from him after Gottlieb stomped off impatiently. And sharing a bedroom, they often talked in the dark… Isaac was comfortable, like having a firm rock to lean against. But now, with Patrick on the scene… Why did Isaac have to get mixed up in this anyway? Hadn't he boasted about how his great-grandparents had fled to Upper Canada back at the time of the American Revolution because they were against fighting? And how even further back they'd left Europe rather than let the young men of the family be pressed into the armies of the German princelings who were forever fighting one another? The night Isaac said he was joining up was the only time Liam had ever seen Gottlieb's wrath turned on his son. "War is wrong…always!" Gottlieb thundered, but Isaac stood his ground. "Not to protect my home," Isaac stated flatly and had gone upstairs to pack. Was that true? Would I do that? Liam wondered. Was that what Da had been doing? And of course this is Isaac's home. If it were my home, what would I do?

"Look, Liam!"

Liam followed her pointing finger. Fifteen

minutes of brisk walking had brought them to the lake shore. In the fields just back of the beach, rows and rows of white canvas bell tents had been erected to house the volunteer troops. Up and down the tent-lined streets soldiers stood or lounged on little camp stools chatting, polishing boots, buffing up brass buttons or oiling rifles.

Lucky them, Liam thought, gazing around. Right in the midst of bustle and chatter, with things happening. He felt a thump on his shoulder and turned just as Rebecca dropped her basket to fling her arms around Isaac.

"Hello, little sister," he shouted, lifting her off her feet to swing her around. Liam stood grinning at them. He could never get over the incongruity of Gottlieb's square face on this exuberant young man of seventeen.

"What have you got in those baskets, then?" Isaac demanded as he set Rebecca on her feet again.

"Are you more interested in what I've brought than in seeing me?"

"Well, I saw you two weeks ago, didn't I?" he teased. "What I saw last night was a rotten dinner and I hope you and Aunt Thirza have saved me from the same fate tonight."

"There's gratitude for you!" Rebecca

pretended to be cross.

"Isn't that what you came for? To save me from death by army rations?" He twitched the linen tea-towel off the basket Liam had set down. "Aunt Thirza's best sausages! Wonderful. You're a lifesaver." He grinned and Liam thought, Yes, that's what's wrong at the foundry…no Isaac.

"Well, come on, you two. Have a look at what we're doing today. And we'll take these with us," Isaac said, hefting the basket Liam had been carrying. "Home-cooked food wouldn't last two seconds around this lot." Talking non-stop, he led them through the rows of tents again, out to the fields.

"You see those rifles over their shoulders?" Isaac pointed out a platoon being drilled by a sergeant. "Dead useless. Just for show."

"What!"

"No ammunition! They're short of it. Every man jack of us sleeping within arm's reach of our rifles and not one of us able to fire the damned things."

"Isaac!" Rebecca gasped. "Your language."

"Just think of it, Liam," Isaac continued, ignoring his sister's outrage. "Seventeenth of March. Attack expected any minute. Sentries along the beach on twenty-four-hour watch.

There I am in the dead of night, marching up and down, eyes peeled for those bastards creeping across the ice…"

"Isaac! What Aunt Thirza is going to say about your language!"

"…and damned if I'd know what to do with it if one of those…"

Rebecca clapped her hands over her ears.

"…those scallywags," he shouted at her, laughing uproariously, "had waved his little green flag under my very nose. I'd never fired the"—he winked at Liam—"blessed thing until this morning, when someone in charge finally decided to give us a little practice. Hell of a kick they've got. My shoulder feels like it's been belted by a sledgehammer." He winked at Liam over his sister's head. "What's happening at home?"

Words tumbled into Liam's mind. I've a cousin come from Ireland, a soldier. He's been looking for me particularly. He needs help with a special mission. He blushed even as he thought the words. Was that what Patrick meant to him? Someone to boast about — a way to show that he, Liam, was important too? He caught Rebecca staring at him. "Oh, you know," he said lamely, "same as usual."

"Boring, eh? Well, let me tell you, it's not

exactly a barrel of laughs in this place, either."

Liam raised his eyebrows in surprise. "What about that, then? Looks pretty exciting." He nodded towards a far field where a sergeant was bellowing at his platoon. As they watched, one line of soldiers fired, then dropped to their knees to reload. The group behind ran ahead of them, then stopped to fire. Close by them a corporal was shouting, "Squad — will fix bayonets. Fix!" over and over as his squad whipped the sword-like weapons out of their belts and jammed them onto their rifles. "Looks pretty exciting to me."

"Yeah, well, can't go by what you see. Now take that one over there. Try crossing him if you want nastiness. Why just yesterday…" He caught sight of his sister staring at him wide-eyed and swallowed the rest of his sentence. "Tell you later."

"What do you mean, you'll tell him later?" Rebecca demanded.

"Soldier's talk," he teased. "Not fit for little girls."

Rebecca's eyes glittered with anger but she pursed her lips primly and said, "In that case, it's not fit for little boys, either."

"Cat," her brother said amiably. "Don't sharpen your claws on Liam."

Rebecca had her mouth open when a voice interrupted them. "What's this, then? Food?" A young man in uniform, his tunic unbuttoned at the neck, pillbox hat under one arm, sauntered up. "Let's see," he demanded.

"Hands off, Peterson!" Isaac whipped the larger basket out of reach.

Liam recognized under the navy tunic Thad Peterson, the son of Daniel Peterson, the carpenter and cabinet maker in Port Colborne.

"Hello, O'Brien. You the beast of burden today?" Thad flicked a careless hand towards the basket Liam had taken from Rebecca.

"You'd better get a move on," he said to Isaac. "Parade in ten minutes. Old fizzywhiskers will have your..." He looked at Rebecca. "...um...your you-know-what for garters if you're late again."

"Good-bye, you two," Isaac said scooping up the second basket. "Thanks for the grub."

The two young men swaggered off. Liam felt a sudden spurt of anger towards Isaac. Turning his back like that. So much for friendship. Well, just wait. Only twenty-four hours now. Twenty-four hours and I'll have something exciting, too. I'll show them!

CHAPTER

FIVE

By supper time the next evening Liam was feeling uneasy. All very well to say "Meet me," he thought, pushing a potato around his plate, but how does Patrick expect me to do it? Good-bye, everybody. I'm off to meet my cousin, the Fenian! A little snort of laughter escaped and he quickly turned it into a dry cough. Out of the corner of his eye he caught Rebecca looking at him, so he hunched over his plate, stuffing his last piece of potato into his mouth.

I don't have to account for every second of my time, he argued with himself. But in such a small household everyone usually knew where the others were and what they were doing. Still, he was known for wandering off with only his flute or a book for company. But not with dark coming on. The problem chased itself like a dog on a treadmill, until Gottlieb's voice broke in.

"Boy, there is for you an errand to do." Liam's mind snapped to attention. Rebecca, removing dishes to the kitchen, paused to listen. "At the Town Hall tomorrow will be a meeting. Tell the Hansens and the Snyders that without fail will I be there."

"A meeting? About what, Papa?"

"About something that concerns the Snyders and the Hansens and myself, daughter," her father replied. The tone was quiet but Rebecca didn't argue. Maybe I'll figure it out from the replies, Liam thought. Be fun to know something Rebecca doesn't... Besides, the road to the Snyders' goes right past... He ran for the door, scooping his jacket off the hook as he went.

"Right. I'm off," he called back over his shoulder. What a piece of luck! No more agonizing. This meeting with Patrick was meant. What clearer sign was ever given a body?

By the time he'd delivered the message, it was dark. He loped towards Snyders' back wood lot, words singing in his head: Something wonderful is going to happen, something wonderful... What was that? Liam stood, silent and still, listening. He glanced behind him, then jumped as fingers squeezed his elbow. There, so close that Liam could feel the warmth of his breath, stood Patrick. He could sense rather than see the grin as Patrick said softly, "And isn't that the dandy man not to go shouting out and spoiling the peace and quiet of the night. 'Tis surely a fine conspirator you'll make!"

Conspirator? A pang of apprehension shot through Liam. "Patrick?" He laughed a little shakily. "Where did you come from so suddenly?"

"A trick of the light, me dear boy." Before Liam could question this cryptic remark, Patrick was urging him over the road towards the fence that snaked along the roadway. "Here's me little hiding place. Just hop this fence and we'll be safe as ferrets down a foxhole."

When they'd settled themselves on a fallen log a dozen yards into the wood lot, Patrick turned and smiled at Liam. "So! You've come."

"I've come," Liam agreed but that word "conspirator" niggled at him.

"And you've been giving thought to what I said?"

"You didn't say much," Liam pointed out warily.

"But you have come."

"Because we're cousins, Patrick. Because you're the only kin I have this side of the Atlantic." And, he added to himself, because I can't stand the foundry any more — people who aren't my people, who don't understand...

"Kinship!" Patrick's voice interrupted his thoughts. "Ah, and what could be a better reason than that? Is it not blood ties have kept Irishmen loyal to the land for two hundred years of black oppression? Delighted I am, Liam, to be the one to welcome you back into the fold. Wasn't it me own mother wrote, 'He's been taken, Patrick. He'll grow up in the land of the enemy. We've lost him forever.' "

"Taken? I wasn't taken!" Liam looked sharply at Patrick. What was he suggesting? "My father came for me as soon as he was able. And it wasn't safe for him to stay in Ireland."

Patrick's expression was as bland as cream. "And is that not the very point I'm making, cousin? A loyal Irishman hunted out of his own country. And did he not tell you why?"

"Yes. Yes, I know about the potatoes rotting in the fields and whole families forced into the workhouse when their cattle were taken for debts." Let's not go on about it, he thought crossly, but wasn't surprised when Patrick persisted.

"And the secret societies, did you not hear about them? How men like your father and mine met secretly because it was treason even to discuss how bad things were?"

"But they didn't..." Liam hesitated, sorting out those old stories. "They didn't just discuss things," he finished softly.

"True for you, me boy. They were men back then. And if helping the poor folk meant dressing up like the Molly Maguires and stealing the cattle back from the sheriff or waylaying the squire and teaching him a lesson, they weren't afraid to do it."

Liam's heart beat faster. Yes, they did go out and make things happen.

"Your father had to flee the country and my father was hanged because a pack of Englishmen are determined to keep our Irish brothers slaves on their own land. Hasn't there just been a mighty war to free the slaves in America? Hasn't that great man, Abraham Lincoln, said there shall be no more slaves? And isn't Ireland all but full of slaves?" Patrick's voice was soft but insistent. "'Twas our fathers died that the Cause might live, Liam. And 'tis you and I that have a sacred duty to see they did not die in vain."

Liam saw his father spitting blood from the lung that had been torn apart by an English bullet. "But," he insisted stubbornly, "that's behind us now. Anyway, there's nothing I can do here."

"And if I could show you something? Something that only you could do? Something so important that without it all might be lost and good men will have died in vain?"

Goose bumps prickled along Liam's arms. Something only he could do? "Why here? Who are you going to fight? What good is this little bit of Canada to the Cause?"

"Is Canada not a creature of the English? And are the English not our enemies? True for you, cousin, 'tis a long way from Ireland. And what we meant for this grand army we've trained was to take ship for Ireland and sweep her clean of her oppressors. To grind down those who've done the grinding down." Patrick's voice, never raised above a whisper, was as icy as a March rain.

Liam shivered.

"The first ship we sent was captured by the enemy," Patrick continued. "When we've raised more money... But we can't wait any longer to show the English we mean business. They'll take notice this time."

Liam's throat tightened. Oh, to be part of this. But... "I'm not a soldier like you."

"Not like me, 'tis true — but a soldier none the less. We all do our part with the weapons we've got."

"What weapons do I have?" Liam thought of the hands that had already let him down in the bell-making.

"A quick eye. And an unquestioned position behind enemy lines."

Enemy lines? Liam frowned. "The foundry?"

"Aye. And the village and the army camp."

"How can those be enemy lines?" And who is the enemy? Gottlieb? Maybe. Isaac? No! Rebecca? Aunt Thirza?

Patrick's voice, soft but insistent, cut into his thoughts. "Are they not on British territory? And are the British not the oppressors? And are you, as a loyal Irishman born and bred, not on the side of justice and of the Cause? Of course you are! Your father's son couldn't be anywhere else."

Liam felt himself lifted up as though on a swell of music. "Yes, Patrick."

"Ah, Liam, didn't I know there was a stout, loyal heart in you? But it needs more than, 'yes,

Patrick'. It requires a solemn oath."

An oath?

"And didn't I take this same oath," Patrick continued, "when I was not a year older than yourself. I was in America by then. The war was a month old and I'd just signed up with the Irish Brigade. Four years of hell that war brought me but I knew I had to learn my trade — soldiering. Not for America — for Ireland! For the Cause! And that's what I'm asking you to be, Liam — a soldier for the Cause. Will you swear, cousin? Will you be a soldier for the Cause?"

"Y-yes. Yes, Patrick." The words burst out of him. All doubts were swept away. "I will swear."

The three-cornered smile was back and Patrick's eyes blazed triumphantly. "And isn't that me own true cousin!" Then the smile vanished, his eyes became sombre and his voice solemn. "Now then, repeat after me: I, Liam O'Brien, in the presence of Almighty God…"

Liam took a deep breath. "…do solemnly swear allegiance to the Irish Republic, and that I will do my utmost, at every risk, while life lasts, to defend its independence and integrity; and finally that I will yield implicit obedience in all things not contrary to the laws of God, to the commands of my superior officers. So help me God."

He had begun the oath in a voice shaking with fright. He ended on a note of steady confidence. He had chosen.

"Let me be telling you about the brotherhood." Patrick's voice came briskly out of the darkness. "Secrecy's the big thing. Until the moment to strike, our enemies must be left complacent and comfortable. We've Fenian brothers in places you'd never expect — Toronto...Hamilton. But 'tis here we've need of a good pair of eyes and a sharp pair of ears, Liam." He paused. "Your ears. Your eyes."

Something only I can do! "What do you need to know, cousin?"

"Little things. Things that might seem unimportant to you, but for us could fill the missing piece of a picture. That camp close by Port Colborne, now. What might be going on down there?"

"Nothing, really," Liam began doubtfully, then suddenly he remembered. He had a wonderful piece of information! "The soldiers — they've hardly any ammunition." Liam was stuttering, so anxious was he to offer up his one treasure to his hero. "And what's more, most of them don't even know how to fire the rifles." Then — oh, God, he thought, Isaac! What have I done?

"Indeed! Well done, cousin!"

It won't matter, Liam told himself. How can it matter?

"Now, me boy, for your first assignment. We've need of a watchman. That tower on top of the foundry. You've no trouble getting into it, you said? And you've a spyglass?"

"Yes, but what shall I watch for?"

"Anything at all about the countryside. Comings and goings on the railway. What the militia do when they're on manoeuvres. That sort of thing."

The airy vagueness in Patrick's voice annoyed Liam. Hadn't he just shown he had important information? "Is that all?" he asked, knowing he sounded disappointed, even petulant.

"Ah, I'm almost forgetting. I've a delivery for you to make. A week — perhaps two — from today there'll be a parcel left — where?" He peered through the darkness to the fence they had clambered over. The posts that held it up were encased in cribs of rock. "There!" he said, waving to the nearest one. " 'Twill be your first work for the Cause, to deliver the parcel

72

left in the crib where and when the instructions say."

"And that's all? I'm to be nothing but a messenger?"

"Indeed and you're not just a messenger." Liam felt Patrick's arm around his shoulder, the voice soft in his ear. "Here's us desperately needing to preserve our secret. And there's you going up and down the town about your business. And who's to ask what the small parcel under your arm might be? Now isn't that a mission to be carried out by yourself and no one else, I ask you?" The arm tightened around his shoulder. "Never you be doubting your worth to us, cousin. A blind, deaf beast we are, feeling our way into this peninsula. 'Tis our eyes and ears you'll be. And just at the beginning, our feet as well. Now isn't that a grand thing I'm asking of you — to be the eyes and ears of the Cause?"

Liam felt the last prick of uneasiness dissolve. "I'll do my best for you, Patrick," he vowed. "My hand on it." He put his hand out and felt it grasped.

"There's a grand man you are. Now..." The voice turned brisk. "...time to be off. But one last thing..." Patrick's eyes glittered black in the moonlight. "Pay heed to what I say to you,

Liam O'Brien. Ireland we must have. And cursed be the hand and withered the arm that will not strike a blow to gain it!"

CHAPTER

SIX

"Liam, Liam! You'll never guess! The most exciting news!"

Liam didn't look up as Rebecca came flying into the shop. *Two more minutes of quiet, that's all I need,* he thought, taking his foot off the treadle as he swung the burnishing wheel away. The bell, held fast in the padded vise on the workbench before him, glowed like freshly poured taffy.

"Liam!"

"What, then?" He took a soft cloth and ran it over the gleaming bronze. *This one's good. Really good! This time Gottlieb will say so.*

"The meeting! Guess what it was about."

"D'ye think I've the second sight, then?" Liam placed the bell carefully on a shelf. "How could I possibly guess?" And why should I care, he thought. Nothing to do with me.

"I'll give you a hint. Bells. Or rather…" She pirouetted around the room, her skirts swirling wide, raising little puffs of dust. "…a particular bell. One as big as… as big as this." She interlaced her fingers and hooped her raised arms in a circle. "Imagine!"

I remember, Liam thought, those plans Gottlieb was showing Mr. Hansen.

"And listen to this!" Rebecca was twirling about the gloomy room as the words tumbled out. "All the neighbours are taking up a subscription to pay for it. It's to be hung in a new belfry on top of the Township Hall and rung the day we celebrate Confederation!"

"Celebrate what?" Then he remembered his father talking about some great plan to unite all the British colonies, to make one country of the four.

"The bell's to have a special message cast on it. But even better, think of this, Liam — for all eternity it will say: Made by Gottlieb Hahn!"

Liam clamped another bell into the vise. "What it will say, you little ignoramus, is *G. Hahn me fecit*. They always inscribe bells in

Latin. And don't get your hopes up — the papers say Confederation isn't going to happen."

"You spoilsport! I'll never tell you anything again!"

Liam, in the act of tightening the vise with a deft, satisfied twist, glanced up. Rebecca's face was stormy, the excitement wiped away. Somewhere inside him a voice said, "What a boy it is for being cross. Now don't be always spoiling things, Liam." How often had his aunt said that to him?

"Sorry," he muttered gruffly, then felt a prickle of annoyance at the surprised look on Rebecca's face. "What else, then?" he asked to make peace. "Did nothing else happen at the meeting?"

Rebecca took a deep breath and unclenched her fists. "There's to be a barrel kept in the shop for collecting copper and brass. Anyone who has brass buttons or broken candlesticks or anything like that can donate them and that way we'll all be a real part of the bell. And of course we'll have to be on the lookout for pedlars coming through. Papa says we'll need nearly two hundred pounds of metal for such a big bell. He might even have to go to Buffalo or get some shipped in from Cleveland. But of course everyone would rather the metal come from here since the bell is for Confederation."

As she paused for breath, the shop door behind them opened. Gottlieb came in, shrugging himself out of his good cloth coat, with Aunt Thirza right behind him.

"Really, Gottlieb," she scolded as he tossed the coat onto a hook. "A fine mess that will be if it's hung up in all this dust and smoke." She swept the coat up and sailed on through the shop towards the back door. "Come along, Rebecca. You have just enough time to finish the bills before we start supper."

Rebecca made a face as she followed her aunt, but Liam knew she liked entering sales in the copperplate hand she had learned in his father's school. The women of the household had always kept the business accounts, leaving Gottlieb and Isaac free to get on with the work of the foundry. Thirza had gallantly taken it on when her sister-in-law died, but she was delighted to discover that Rebecca had a natural talent for balancing income and disbursements. Now, two years after Thirza had taught her how, Rebecca was long past being an apprentice bookkeeper. And even though Liam had no head for numbers, he could understand the satisfaction the neatly balanced rows of figures gave Rebecca.

Not so different from me with these bells. He looked at his morning's work — the row of gleaming bells that lined the shelf above the burnishing wheel — and thought, I know they're good. This time he'll say so.

Gottlieb rolled up his sleeves and tied his leather apron on. Carrying one of the bells to the window, he scrutinized it in the strong afternoon light. Liam knew what he was looking for — rough spots missed by the abrasive wheel, gouges where the wheel had been held in one spot too long. The final grinding and polishing tuned the bell. Too much left on here, not enough taken off there and it wouldn't ring true.

'Tis as good a job as anyone could do, Liam thought fiercely, and he'd better say so.

Gottlieb righted the bell and tapped it with a small leather mallet. It sang sweetly through the room, each of its five notes clear and pure. Liam closed his eyes and revelled in the harmony of overtones and undertones. "So!" Gottlieb nodded as he replaced the bell. "All is smooth, the sound is true. The bell is in tune with itself." Liam could hardly believe his ears. At last. At last... "For once," his master continued drily, "it would seem you have kept your mind where it belongs."

The elation turned sour in Liam's mouth. Was there never to be a "well done"? Was it always to be a grudging "not bad" or the more usual "it could be better"? Isaac would just have grinned and replied, "*Naturlich*, Father!" but then Isaac wasn't an orphan taken in out of pity. No, not pity. My father paid an apprentice fee. I'm worth money to Gottlieb! He fought the impulse to snatch the bell and hurl it through the nearest window.

Oblivious to Liam's mood, Gottlieb moved on to the furnace. "This afternoon will we melt down the scrap in this barrel so that tomorrow we can cast the findings for Mr. O'Halloran at the ship chandler's. And we will need the other barrel. Bring it also." He paused for a moment as though trying to decide something, then said, "Rebecca has told you about the bell for the Township Hall?"

Lost in his own thoughts, Liam almost missed the question. "Yes. Yes, she told me," he muttered. Then, to himself as he trudged into the back room, "Don't know what difference it makes to me."

"Already is the rough design accomplished!" Gottlieb announced.

We're sounding very German today, Liam thought. Wonder what's up?

Once, when he and his father had been walking home from Sunday dinner at the Hahns', he'd made fun of that Germanic angularity in Gottlieb's speech.

"Liam, Liam," his father had chided. "And how do you think our speech sounds to him?" Liam had gaped. How could their speech sound strange? By then the schoolmaster was in full flight. "The Hahns came from the German settlements down in Pennsylvania. When the American Revolution broke out, they left a prosperous farm and foundry to resettle up here."

"Why?" Liam asked and then was sorry, as his father continued to lecture.

"They were grateful to the British king — George the Third it was back then — for giving them a home after they had to flee persecution in their own country. Yes, we have a lot in common with the Hahns," he continued in response to Liam's look of surprise. "And if Gottlieb's speech hearkens back to his German forebears — well, all honour to him for valuing his past. No matter now long you live here, Liam, Ireland will always be on your tongue."

Gottlieb's voice roused Liam from his musings. "Yes! Tonight yet will I begin the exact calculations."

He's excited about this bell, Liam realized. That's why he's gone all German. Well, well! Then he remembered his own grievances and his thoughts turned sour again. Don't count your chickens, Master Hahn. Confederation hasn't happened yet.

* * *

Whatever Gottlieb thought about Confederation, he was engrossed with the township bell. Every evening he placed the coal-oil lamp in the centre of the kitchen table, then lined up pen and inkwell, ruler, dividers and compasses before settling in to draft the next aspect of the bell. Precise measurements marked off each section — so deep for the sound bow, three times that for the waist, a certain percentage of the whole for the shoulder. The diameter was to be twenty-two inches and he was working out on paper specific proportions — the exact height, thickness and curvature of the sides to achieve the most resonant sound.

Often Liam sat in the warm kitchen playing softly on his flute, with Aunt Thirza and Rebecca sewing nearby, watching as the meticulous drawings flowed from Gottlieb's pen. He pictured the small bells they cast in the shop, each size with its mould ready and waiting. Years ago, when those moulds were made, did this much art and mathematics go into their fashioning?

His thoughts drifted to his own puzzle — the parcel Patrick had promised. Was it just a dream? Was I hallucinating for lack of food? Then he would catch himself playing "Fionnuala's Song." No! It really happened. But where is Patrick? Why no word, no sign?

April rains washed away the last of the snow, then drummed the roadways into ankle-deep bogs. Damp invaded the house so that every sheet felt clammy despite Rebecca's smoothing with the warming pan. Even the walls seemed to sweat. In the foundry, soot from the fire smeared like ink on hands and faces. "Ach, such weather!" Gottlieb would exclaim as the wood hissed and popped in the stove, making more smoke than heat.

Every so often one of the household would squish and squelch into town for supplies or down to the military camp. The mood had turned sour there as well.

"Not a damned thing happening!" Isaac exploded at Liam one day. "With all I want to do at home! I would have had my little steam engine finished and running by now."

"'Tis purgatory," Liam agreed. They were huddled in Isaac's tent to get out of the cold drizzle. Liam inched his camp stool away from the sagging canvas wall and its wooden legs scratched lines in the earthen floor. The wet-wool smell of the uniforms caught at his throat and he coughed. "What a way to live. Why are they keeping you here?"

"Whoever tells a soldier anything? Rumour has it the orders come from John Macdonald himself. God knows where he gets his information but he seems to think that one of these days we're going to fight the Fenians. With what, I'd like to know? Our two whole bullets apiece?" Isaac hooted, and his square face lit up in fleeting amusement.

Liam, watching him, suddenly remembered, I told Patrick there were no bullets. What if the Fenians really do invade? It'll be Isaac out there on the battlefield — maybe even facing Patrick. And with nothing to defend himself! Liam's stomach contracted painfully. No, nothing will happen, he told himself. Even the newspapers say it's nothing but a tempest in a teapot. Then why, a little inner voice demanded, why is the government keeping hundreds of soldiers waiting around in the mud and rain? Still, there's been no sign from Patrick. Perhaps the Fenians have given up — gone away and Patrick with them. Immediately Liam's stomach settled. Why? Why am I so relieved? Am I a coward, afraid of a fight? Isaac obviously isn't and he doesn't even have enough bullets for a fair fight! If I were a true soldier for the Cause, he reasoned, watching Isaac scrape mud from the sole of one boot, I would be delighted to find the enemy's weaknesses. The thought made him shiver. But isn't it, after all, my father's cause, my cousin's cause, my kinfolks' cause? Then why am I sitting here? He looked at Isaac, who had crossed one leg over the other to get at the wedge of mud caught between heel and sole.

"Ah, what's the use?" Isaac said suddenly, throwing his knife down. "What's the use of any of this? Come on. We'll get some coffee."

Liam followed him into the rain, glad to push the troubling thoughts away — but the respite was temporary. As day dragged after dreary day the arguments nagged at him, troubled his sleep, roughened his tongue until he and Rebecca were snapping at each other like yappy little dogs. And everywhere he turned, Gottlieb loomed.

"No! Not that way!" he thundered for what seemed the thousandth time that month as

Liam tamped moulding earth into a wooden frame. "It must be even all over, the pressure. Here, I will myself do it." He pushed Liam aside. "A hundred orders we have and my *dummkopf* apprentice cannot properly a simple mould fill."

Liam clenched his teeth. I'm fed up with this, he thought, then heard himself saying, "I did it the way you showed me." He glared across the workbench at his master. I'm standing my ground this time, he decided even as he saw the black eyebrows snap together.

"So! A know-nothing apprentice wishes to teach me, Gottlieb Hahn, master founder, how to do my work?"

"I did it the way you said," Liam muttered. He could feel his chin trembling. I will not back down, he told himself. I will not!

"Bah! Not so. Did I say here punched down and there so loose I can flick it out with my fingernail? What happens beneath this? Air bubbles around the form. A spoiled pour. Worse yet, a deadly accident!"

A chill ran though Liam. In his mind he heard the sudden sizzle of hot metal hitting those air pockets, that damp earth — then the explosion. He hadn't actually seen a mould explode but he been told over and over how easily it could happen — how devastating the injuries. His throat tightening, he looked again. Yes, he admitted to himself, the spots do look soft. But then, I'm not finished. What does he expect when I'm only half done? "You didn't give me enough time. I was just after getting to those parts."

"Time? It is not time you lack. It is care. It is method. Look!" The master founder seized the wooden flask, clamping it to the workbench with his left hand while he began tamping the earth with the wedge-shaped ram in his right hand. "From this corner you start and work methodically — so — not a bit here and a bit there." As he spoke he worked the ram across the length of the flask then back again in rows as straight as a ruled edge. "What kind of foundryman will you become if you have no method?"

"And why didn't you ever tell me that before — about method?" Liam blurted out. "And what does it matter to you, anyway? You don't really care about me. You were paid to have me."

Gottlieb glared, amazement and then fury gathering in his expression. "So! This is what you think? Without the money I would not take the boy? Do you think it is nothing to me that a careless apprentice ruins my work — and endangers life in the bargain? I would not take you for money or for friendship if I did not think you could a foundryman make. And now what am I to think? All is carelessness and waste. Go! Clean up the back room. The rest will I do myself."

Liam slammed into the back room. It was always the same with Gottlieb: "This is not good enough. Go. I will myself do it." With his own father it would have been: "Now, Liam, whatever would you be doing here? Let's just be starting again and have another try at it." And they'd sit and work together through some tricky problem in arithmetic or a particularly awkward piece of Latin translation. Of course, he'd liked doing the things his father taught him — parsing an English sentence or sorting out the exact meaning of a Latin phrase. "I've nothing to leave you but my learning, Liam," he'd said that terrible summer as he grew visibly weaker and weaker. "You haven't enough yet to run this school and I'll not have you scraping out a living in one of those disgraceful backwoods schools. I've arranged something that I think will work better for you." Well, you were wrong, Da.

Somehow they trudged through April. Gottlieb seemed less explosive and actually took the time every so often to explain calmly why a piece of work didn't measure up to his expectations. Liam, for his part, gave himself a mental shake whenever he found himself drifting off into daydreams about Patrick and the parcel.

On the seventeenth of April, the Canal was officially opened for the season. Liam felt a strange excitement bubble through him when he opened the front door one day and saw, in the distance, the top of a mast. From then on, whenever he had a few spare minutes, he would squirrel himself into the cupola and watch as ship after ship was towed along the canal. Reading their flags made him feel restless. *I wonder where I'd be by now if I had run away that night? I should have! All that's keeping me here is Patrick, and God knows where he is. Why doesn't the message come?*

On the last day of April, when the sun finally lit up a blue sky, Gottlieb decided to inspect the roof of the Township Hall. To hold a two-hundred-pound bell and its belfry, it needed to be strong. Liam was sent to fetch Mr. Snyder and Mr. Hansen. As he walked down the road he thought, I'll give Patrick one more chance. If he hasn't left me a message, that's it — forget Patrick.

At the fence post by Snyder's wood lot, he crossed the fingers of both hands, then jumped the ditch. The rocks in the log cribbing were damp. A ribbon of moss threaded its way in and out of the pile. That's never been touched in weeks, Liam thought, disappointment rising sourly in his throat. He kicked sharply at the crib and a flat, greyish parcel tumbled out. From under the edge of the oiled cloth a corner of white paper showed. Liam twitched it out. Fergus Whelan, c/o O'Halloran's Ship Chandlers, Port Colborne, it said.

Is this it, then, Liam wondered. No message. But it must be from Patrick. He looked at the address again, black and bold — like an order. Captain to soldier. Do this! But do I want to do this? He heard his father's voice saying, "A man is judged by his actions, Liam. Always be honourable in your actions." And his father had been a Young Irelander. Besides, he, Liam, had already sworn an oath. And anyway, was delivering a parcel such a big thing? He tucked it under his arm and started down the road.

For two days the parcel plagued Liam. How urgently does it need to be delivered, how soon will I get a half day off, how safely can I keep it hidden? The first night he tucked it into the straw ticking under his mattress but every time he turned over, its sharp corners prodded him awake. Then, at breakfast, Aunt Thirza announced that spring cleaning would begin in a week. The parcel would have to be outside the house before that turmoil began. But where?

Liam was stacking wood along the side wall of the foundry, his mind running over possible hiding spots, when Mr. Hansen's wagon rattled into the driveway.

"Good day t'ye, boy. Have you heard the news? The militia's being disbanded."

Gottlieb closed the foundry at noon. "We will go, all of us, to bring Isaac home," he announced and went to hitch up the delivery wagon. "And since we are passing by, we will drop off O'Halloran's order."

At last — my chance, Liam thought, bounding up the stairs to snatch the parcel from under his mattress. He tucked it firmly into his waistband under his coat and pelted out again.

As Aunt Thirza settled herself on the seat, Liam vaulted up beside Rebecca on the tail of the wagon. Gottlieb clucked to the horses and the wagon rattled down the lane. They lurched onto the road and Liam had to grab with both hands at the railing to keep from being jolted off. The parcel shifted under his coat and he tensed his left arm to keep it clamped to his side. He glanced at Rebecca, but for once she had no interest in what he was doing. Holding tightly to the railing on her side she was singing — quietly, so that Aunt Thirza wouldn't scold her for unladylike behaviour, but joyously — her own words to an American army song they had heard over and over during the long Civil War to the south.

"When Isaac comes marching home again,
hurrah, hurrah…"

CHAPTER

SEVEN

"That will be the last of them, Mr. O'Halloran."

As Liam handed over the manifest, he glanced out the window of the ship chandler's. The emptied delivery wagon by the front door gave a lurch and rolled forward. Rebecca waved. Good! They were on their way. He squeezed his elbow against his side, feeling for the little parcel. Still tight in the waistband. He'd been sure it was going to slither down his leg when they were off-loading the kegs. He leaned on the counter while the shopkeeper checked the contents of the kegs and boxes against the numbers on the list. Five minutes to do that, he thought, then I'll hand over the parcel and be off to the camp myself. Things, he decided contentedly, are working out.

Idly he stared around the shop. A sign painted in black curlicued letters announced: Complete Outfitting and Provisioning for Captain and Crew. Charts, Cordage and Canvas. Complete's the word, Liam thought. By his elbow lay a pile of marlin spikes supplied by Gottlieb. A gleaming brass compass hung on gimbals in a wooden case. Shelves were stacked with tins of snuff and plugs of chewing tobacco. To pass the time, he started to count the rope tails that hung down from spindles anchored to the ceiling. His eyes followed them down the long wall, then stopped. From the farthest corner of the room, two black button eyes stared at him over the bowl of a huge pipe. A gnome of a man was perched cross-legged on top of a barrel of oakum.

"G'day," a gravelly voice said around the stem of the pipe. "Nice kind of a day out there, inn't?"

"Aye, that it is, sir." The eyes made him shift uncomfortably. He locked his elbow tightly over the parcel.

"Bean't you Founder Hahn's young Irish 'prentice?"

"I am that, sir." Liam looked more closely at

94

the figure hunched snugly on top of the barrel. Stained baggy trousers. Shabby black jacket. Never seen him before, Liam decided.

"Aye, well, I can see you don't remember me — Alfred J. Wister, Dealer in Divers Metals and Scrap, at your service, young master."

Wisht, thought Liam, there's a fancy title for a junk pedlar. But he replied politely, "I don't just recall you to mind, sir. 'Twas a different man through the last time."

"Prolly, prolly. I'm usually east of here." He sucked on his pipe again. "I'd take it kindly if you'd just tell Mister Hahn that Alf Wister'll be coming through in a day or two with a choice lot of copper and tin. I unnerstand as how he's scouting out metal for that jeezly great bell they're wanting to whack up top o' the Township Hall?"

Liam was about to reply when the chandler called to him. "All accounted for," he said. "Here's your receipt. Now if you'll just be helping me heft these kegs around the counter like a good lad, you can be on your way. Down to the camp, is it? Quite the commotion, what with everyone moving out."

As he tilted a keg to wheel it across the floor, Liam said, "There's something else, Mr. O'Halloran, something I was asked to leave with you." He reached under his coat and brought out the parcel. "'Tis to be called for by a man named Fergus Whelan."

"Fergus Whelan?" The shopkeeper straightened abruptly and the keg rocked back onto its base. "Now what would you be knowing about the likes of Fergus Whelan?" he demanded sharply.

Liam was glad he could answer truthfully, "I wouldn't be knowing him from Adam, sir. I was just asked to pass this on t'you."

"And who would be asking such a thing of you, then?"

"Just — just someone I met on the road." Liam heard himself stammer over the lie. He took a quick breath to calm himself and continued, his speech getting more Irish by the second. "Didn't he say he hadn't the time to come all the way into town and would I just be dropping it off as a favour to a countryman?"

"Yes, well, you be careful who you're doing favours for, me lad. I doubt your father, rest his soul, would want his son having any truck with the likes of Fergus Whelan. The worst of a bad lot, that one." He tossed the parcel on the counter and turned back to the kegs. "Now just catch a hold of this and let's be getting on with it."

Liam turned to grasp the keg and was startled to find the scrap metal dealer at his elbow. The little man flashed a gap-toothed grin at him and his bright black eyes almost disappeared behind his crinkled cheeks.

"Would you excuse me, sir — I need to be moving these kegs right where you're standing."

The little man skipped out of his way, then leaned casually on the counter, tamping tobacco into his pipe and darting sly glances at the package. Why doesn't he just shove off? Liam gave the next keg an angry jerk.

When the last of the kegs was in place, Liam dusted his hands down the backs of his trousers, tugged his weskit neatly over his waistband and straightened his jacket. "I'll be saying good day, then, Mr. O'Halloran." He backed towards the door, his eyes still on the amiably puffing Alf Wister.

"Now you mind what I said, young Liam. You be giving those navvies a miss," the shopkeeper admonished. "They're bad business, they are. I'm an Irishman myself but I'd give each and every one of them the back of me hand quicker than I'd give them the time of day."

"Yes, sir." Liam backed out of the store. As he turned, a small pane of glass reflected Alf Wister reaching eagerly for the parcel.

Well now you've done it, Liam berated himself as he loped off down the road towards the lake. That nosy little weasel of a man was just dying to find out all about that parcel. Surely Mr. O'Halloran wouldn't be letting him open it even if he does hate this Fergus Whelan, whoever the divil he is? Leaving parcels there is supposed to be just like leaving them at the post office. And what if he tells Gottlieb? Ach well, so what? Surely there's no harm in dropping off a parcel. But what would Patrick have to do with this Fergus if he's as bad as Mr. O'Halloran thinks? It's probably all prejudice because he's a navvie.

It wasn't just Mr. O'Halloran. His father had warned him to steer clear of navvies, too. "Giving the Irish a bad name," he'd said as he and Liam had watched a dozen of them one evening reeling from tavern to tavern. "I know it's a hard life. I'd hate to spend my days plodding along those tow-paths with nothing to do but guide a horse that's dragging a ship — but all this brawling and drinking! No wonder the townsfolk are quick to condemn anyone with a rough Irish brogue."

Including me, Liam thought, remembering back six years to schoolyard taunts when he'd come out with words like "praties" and "crubeen." With his father's educated Dublin accent in his ear, he soon softened his Irish speech, but his name and the red hair he shared with half the navvies around made him feel he was always fighting against that whispered judgement — "good-for-nothing Irish."

Deep in gloomy reflections, he swung along the road. Gradually sounds beat into his thoughts — shouts and the rhythmic thud, thud of wooden mauls on wood. He stood for a moment staring at the confusion before him. Half the tents had been struck, some folded away, others drooping like deflated balloons while their former occupants rolled guy ropes and pulled apart the sectioned centre poles. Soldiers piled the tents and trappings onto wagons that stood amid the clutter, their heavily blinkered horses snorting and stamping at the confusion.

Liam could tell from their uniforms that the soldiers were volunteers. That morning — so they'd heard — the regular militia had entrained for Hamilton, where they would stay as part of the Province of Canada's standing army. The Fenians might still be gathering in Buffalo and other border cities but the authorities just weren't taking them seriously any more. Only last week they'd heard that the Fenian invasion of New Brunswick had completely collapsed after a few hours of strutting and posturing, and the newspapers were crowing: "The Fenian conspiracy has been rendered harmless by the proved imbecility and roguery of its ringleaders... The leaders are without brains, the followers are without character. From such a motley crew we need fear nothing." Obviously Niagara no longer needed defending. Even the volunteers were being sent home.

But were the Fenians a "motley crew" with men the like of Patrick among them? Maybe the politicians were a little too sure of themselves. What was the word for that? Hubris. From the Greek, Da had said, meaning "overweening conceit." And how was hubris punished? The Greek heroes had been struck down by the gods. Well, this was hardly a Greek tragedy. More like a comedy, he mused wryly, looking around the canvas-strewn field.

"Liam!" The Hahns' team and wagon was clattering towards him. Standing in the back, waving his pillbox hat over the heads of his father and aunt, was Isaac. Liam grinned and waved back. Now maybe life would improve.

* * *

The first week Isaac was back in the foundry, Liam was amazed to hear Gottlieb whistling tunelessly under his breath as he chiselled away at the edge of a bell. What's got into him? Must be having Isaac back — or all the work that's getting done. Liam was kept busy hauling pails of coke for the furnace or lugging cordwood to feed the steam engine that pumped the bellows. By the end of each day he was too tired to check the fence post, almost too tired to eat. By the end of the week he noticed another strange sensation. He was feeling discontented again. Nothing interesting to do.

"I'll do that," he heard himself saying one day as Isaac set up the polishing wheel.

"You?"

"I polished while you were away. I did those bells," Liam said defensively, pointing to the shelf where some of the bells still sat.

"Oh, well, it's only trivets. Can't harm those. Have a turn, then, bantam."

Liam felt his face go red. I'll show him! he thought as Isaac shrugged and waved him towards the polishing wheel. An hour later, he had a stack of gleaming circular trivets at his elbow.

"Hey, not bad." Issac's voice cut into the wall of concentration Liam had built around himself. "Don't know as I could do any better myself." Isaac was holding one up to the light of the window. A glow started in the pit of Liam's stomach and flamed right up to the roots of his hair. He knew that Isaac had the same knack with metal as his father. Better even, so Aunt Thirza said, than his older brother Jacob. Liam had only her word for that. Jacob had been killed in an accident the year Liam and his father arrived in Stonebridge. "Don't mention him to my brother," Aunt Thirza had once cautioned Liam. "Gottlieb can't bear to remember that the foundry caused Jacob's death." Still blazoned across the front wall was a sign reading G. Hahn and Sons.

Praise from Isaac meant something, but there was one thing lacking. "I'm still not strong enough to help with a pour," he ventured, almost hoping Isaac would deny it.

"It'll come," Isaac said carelessly. "Can't expect to pour when you've got arms like string beans." Liam turned away but Isaac caught hold of him. "Hey, listen, no one gets their full strength before seventeen. Look at that arm." He made a fist so the muscles of his upper arm rippled and bulged. "Like a piece of string when I was your age. Give you my word. Didn't have the strength of a sausage."

Liam grinned back, comforted but wondering if the passage of three years could make such a difference in *his* muscles.

So involved was he with the work of the shop that Patrick's next appearance came as a shock. He'd been up to the cupola several times to have a look around the countryside but he hadn't been out to check the post in nearly two weeks. His conscience was prodding him. A message might have been waiting for days. But now it wasn't just Rebecca's sharp eyes he had to avoid. There was Isaac, too — what with sharing a bedroom and going off on little jaunts to hunt or fish in their free time — how could he explain an absence to Isaac?

He was mulling over the problem one evening out in the privy. As he was unlatching the door to leave, a melodic whistling started up somewhere close by.

"Patrick?" he breathed into the darkness. "Where are you?"

"In the bushes, cousin. Just be skipping around here for a moment, will ye?"

Liam glanced towards the house. He could see Rebecca and Aunt Thirza silhouetted against the kitchen window. Gottlieb sometimes sat and smoked his pipe in the dark of the veranda but no tell-tale glow showed anywhere along its length. If anyone started in this direction, he'd hear the door squeak. It was dark enough. I'll be no more than a shadow if they look this way, he decided, slipping around the back and into the bushes.

Patrick was sitting on a tree stump, one foot resting on a shadowy black cylinder. "I expected to see you last night. Did you not find my message?"

Liam's throat felt dry. He gave a little cough. "I couldn't get away." He shifted uncomfortably from one foot to the other. "It's much harder now that Isaac's back."

"Now how much use is a messenger who doesn't get messages, I wonder?" Patrick's voice was soft and musing but Liam felt a prickle of unease even though the tone held no hint of menace.

"We're so busy…" he stammered.

"Well, never mind that now. Come farther back here behind the stables so there's no chance we'll be heard." Patrick gestured towards the building that loomed twenty yards behind the house, scooping up his bundle as he spoke. "And have you delivered the parcel I left for you?" Patrick asked when they were safely tucked into a corner of the building.

"I did indeed and just two days after I found it," Liam began eagerly. "We had to go into…"

"Aye, well, the details don't matter. I've another job for you, now." He set a cask on the ground between them. "Oysters. For a friend."

Liam felt a stab of resentment. What was he? — a delivery boy to run social errands? It was just a silly game, this cloak-and-dagger stuff. Why should he bother to run the risk of landing in trouble if anyone found out? "I thought I'd be doing something important."

"Will ye listen to the lad!" the low voice hissed. "And who are you to be deciding what's important and what's not? Ah, Liam, you're so young. Did it never occur to you that it's all of us doing these little things that prepare the way for the important event?"

"But a keg of oysters?"

"Liam, Liam! A soldier obeys orders."

Liam swallowed. "Yes, cousin."

"There now! And as a little reward I'll tell you this — when the hour comes you'll have an important part to play — a very important part indeed. In the meantime I must have this cask taken care of 'til it's needed."

"Is it for Fergus Whelan?"

"And if it is?"

"Mr. O'Halloran at the ship chandler's warned me off him. Said he was a bad sort. He might wonder…"

"And what's to wonder? The man's in the business of forwarding. Anyway, for the moment I'll be needing you to hide it here."

"But if it's oysters…"

"Liam!"

"Yes, cousin." Liam heard the meekness in his voice. Why can't you say what you think? he asked himself angrily. If you don't want to do it, say so.

"Good man." Patrick's voice was soothing. "I knew I wouldn't be having to remind you that you'd sworn a sacred oath. Now, have ye anything else to tell me? What have you seen around and about that might help the Cause?"

A picture of the camp breaking up flashed into Liam's mind. No. Not that. What else? "The regular militia has gone back to Hamilton," he offered reluctantly. Patrick murmured encouragingly and Liam felt drawn to say more. "The volunteers have been disbanded. The camp broke up a week ago."

"Aye, I knew that, the silly spalpeens," Patrick snorted.

"Does that mean there will be an attack?"

Was it alarm or excitement, that little stab of feeling?

"Liam, Liam, you'll know what you need to know when you need to to know it." Then his voice sharpened. "No more talk! They'll be wondering up at the house did you fall down the hole. Now listen carefully. The keg's either to be delivered or to be called for in seven days — on the twenty-ninth of May. One way or another, I'll get a message to you saying what's to be done. See you keep it safe until then." There was a pause and then, "I'm counting on you, cousin."

Are you indeed, Liam thought. Well, this time you've asked the impossible. Where am I supposed to stow something that size? He was about to demand help when he realized he was standing alone. Patrick had vanished and not a sound revealed the direction he had taken.

The stable for tonight, I guess, Liam thought wearily. A week! How can I keep it hidden that long?

CHAPTER

EIGHT

A week, Liam groaned the next day as he shovelled moulding earth into the sieving box. Keep it safe for me, he says. How ever on God's green earth am I to do that? he asked himself for the hundredth time that morning. His stomach growled. Must be nearly dinner time. He squinted across the room at the wall clock. Five to twelve. Two more scoops and I'll quit. Just as he dug the shovel into the pile, he heard the clatter of wheels on the gravelled drive. He glanced out the open doorway. Oh, no. If that isn't the final straw! The name stencilled neatly along the side of the rig pulled up to the door was Alfred J. Wister.

What the divil does he want? Maybe he

opened that parcel. No. Be sensible. Why should he? He's got scrap for sale like any other pedlar. If only he doesn't mention it... "Someone to see you," he called over his shoulder to Gottlieb. The junkman was knotting his reins through the ring on the horsehead hitching post. Liam never looked at that iron pole without remembering that Isaac had cast it when he was only twelve.

"G'day, g'day." Alf Wister stepped into the shop without waiting to be asked. "Well, there you are, young master. Told you I'd be 'round in a bit, dinn't I? And here's the man himself." He wiped a grimy paw down the side of his trousers before holding it out to Gottlieb. "Alfred J. Wister, Metal and Scrap. Heard you was on the lookout for copper and brass. Now I just happen to have a dandy load of the very stuff you need. Casting a rumbustious great bell, there, are yuh? Heard all about it more'n one place." The little man rattled on while Gottlieb stood politely waiting for him to run out of steam.

A bell clanged three times. Alf cocked his head to one side. "Now what's that I hear?" he demanded, having refreshed himself with a lungful of air. "One of your famous bells, if I'm not mistaken." He looked expectantly at Gottlieb.

"The dinner bell," Gottlieb supplied. "Will you break bread with us, Mr. Wister?"

"Why, thankee. Don't mind if I do. Don't mind if I do. Nothing better than talking business after a good meal, I always say."

Damnation, Liam thought, he's just the gabby type to mention that parcel. As the door closed behind the two men, Isaac came whooping out of the back room. "What's the joke?" Liam asked.

"Dinner conversation should be priceless today. Come on, bantling, race you."

Alf Wister was what Liam's father would have called "a powerful talker." Through the soup course and the meat and vegetables and on into the rice pudding, he dominated the conversation, stabbing the air with his fork to make a point, but never missing a dish that passed his way. Prompted by the odd question from Gottlieb, he commented on all the news — local, provincial and beyond.

"Innerestin' them down-easters suddenly decidin' they was on our side," he mused halfway through his bowl of vegetable soup. "One minute they won't touch us with a barge pole. Next minute Confederation's just their cup of tea. Don't feel so independent once someone takes a bash at them, seems like."

"Papers say it's nonsense," Isaac suggested with the air of someone laying kindling on the fire. "Claim the Fenians had no chance of invading New Brunswick from the start."

"Now there you're wrong!" The little man turned from the bowl of potatoes to wave his knife at Isaac. "Take Cornwall. I was there last month when the army stopped that train. Full of Fenians it was. All from Toronto. They had to prod those devils off the cars with their bayonets. How's that for fierce? Don't you unnerestimate them Fenians, young man. New Brunswick — that was just luck! Their bad luck. Our good luck." He paused to swallow the potato wadded in his cheek. "Hear you had some innerestin' developments in this neck of the woods." His tone was casual but he darted avid glances around the table as though greedy for each reaction. As the button eyes lighted on him, Liam blanked all expression from his face but his throat was tight. Was this it? Surely one little package couldn't be considered an interesting development?

Rebecca was staring open-mouthed at their dinner guest. Aunt Thirza looked mildly interested. Gottlieb continued his methodical progress through the carrots on his plate. But Isaac winked at Liam before fanning the flames.

"You certainly pick up a great deal of information on your little excursions, Mr. Wister. What else's happened?" His tone was solemn but Liam could hear the pent-up laughter behind it. Isaac loved the absurd.

But Alf surprised him. "Quite a to-do at that camp down the end of the canal. Madder'n treed cats, they was, when I passed yestiday." Again he scanned the table, sure of a mesmerized audience. "Good bit o' gunpowder's gone missing. Four kegs of it. And the big question is — who'd want it?"

In the moment of stunned silence, Liam had a vision of the oyster keg hidden in Gottlieb's barn. He almost bit his tongue in the effort to make no sound.

Isaac's playful drawl broke the tension. "Surely the question is — who could carry them away? That's quite a load."

"Them little kegs? One under each arm." Alf made hoops of his arms to show how easy it would be. "Two men — boys even."

"Still — four. Heavy going. Need a wagon, I'd think. And something to hide them under. And it would help to be someone who moved around a lot."

Just as Liam realized what Isaac was hinting at, Rebecca smothered a giggle. Gottlieb said,

"Isaac!" reprovingly but his son grinned unrepentantly at the junk dealer.

"Oh ho, young master, I gets yer drift." Alf waggled his fork playfully at Isaac. "No, no. Alfred J. Wister's no thief. Anyway, what use would gunpowder be to me? No, my guess is —" He lowered his voice and peered around the table eagerly. "— my guess is there's Fenian sympathizers in these here parts." The little man beamed proudly into the thunderstruck silence.

Isaac was the first to recover. "Any candidates, Mr. Wister?" he asked, his eyes filled with unholy glee. "We've a stout young Irishman right here." He clapped Liam on the shoulder. "How about him?"

Liam's head swam. Damn Isaac! But the junkman was chuckling. "Young men will have their bit of fun, now won't they? Just wonderin' what you folks had heard — out of curiosity like. Any strangers about?"

"Only yourself, Mr. Wister," Gottlieb said mildly. "Unless the boys have seen someone."

Liam glanced at Isaac. Leave it, he begged silently, but Isaac was like a terrier with a rabbit. "Tell me, Mr. Wister, what need would Fenians have to steal gunpowder so far away from their base? Perhaps they're short on ammunition, like us? That would be a good joke, wouldn't it? We stand facing the enemy and neither side can fire at the other. Maybe I should take my slingshot next time. Or a pea-shooter."

"This is not a matter for jokes, Isaac," Gottlieb interrupted. "And it is not a matter I wish discussed at my dinner table. In this house we do not cast doubt on our neighbours' loyalty, Mr. Wister."

"Just so, just so," Alf agreed hastily, stuffing the last of the mashed turnip into his mouth. "No offence meant, and none taken, I hope."

"Thirza, we will have dessert," Gottlieb said, clearly closing the matter.

When the meal was over and Alf Wister was waiting for Gottlieb to look through his scrap, he raised the subject again. He was leaning on the wheel of his wagon, which stood on a gravelled area at the back of the foundry. Liam and Isaac were clambering over the contents, doing a quick preliminary sort while they waited for Gottlieb, who was in the shop with a customer.

"That there tower, now..." Alf pointed with the stem of his pipe to the cupola on the roof of the foundry. "...wunnerful lookout, that. This flat country — you could see for miles. See the railroads and all them ships coming up the canal, I shouldn't doubt?"

Liam turned away, hoping to discourage the junkman but his heart sank as Isaac answered, "That we can, Mr. Wister. We can see right down to the lake the one way and beyond Ramey's Bend the other way."

"Man with a spyglass, I don't doubt he could sight a man skulking about anywheres along that canal. Might even see his face as clear as I can see you?"

"You seem to have a keen interest in spying, Mr. Wister," Isaac commented.

"Spying? Not me, young sir. Curiosity's the name of my game. Always was curious about the way folks go on. And you'll admit, there's a powerful lot to be curious about these days what with them Irishmen — saving your presence, young master — " this with a nod towards Liam, "them Irishmen skulking about on the border and no one knowing from one day to the next what they're up to."

When Gottlieb appeared at the back door, even Alf knew enough to drop the subject. He tapped his pipe against the side of the wagon, spilling the still-smoking dottle onto the gravel, stamped on it smartly and became, in an instant, the complete man of business. Relief flooded through Liam.

For the next hour, as Gottlieb chose scrap for the bell, Liam and Isaac trotted back and forth between the wagon and the scales that stood just inside the office door. As he lifted and carried, Liam tried to suppress the suspicion that was rapidly becoming a certainty in his mind. In the dark last night he hadn't really had a good look at Patrick's cask. What if…?

When Gottlieb had paid the junk dealer from the strongbox he kept in the office, Alfred J. Wister scrambled back onto his high perch. Rebecca came running out as the little man rattled off down the laneway. Isaac and Gottlieb turned back to the shop but Liam, lost in thought, stood waving with Rebecca until all they could see of the junkman was the dust flung up by his wheels.

"Liam?" Rebecca's voice came from behind his left ear.

He cocked his head to one side but didn't quite turn towards her. "Yes?".

"You went white as the tablecloth when Isaac was joking about your being a Fenian."

"I did not!" Damn. Trust Rebecca to notice.

"I was looking right at you. You — blanched," she pronounced dramatically. "Every single freckle stood out on your face. Are you one of them? I mean," she amended hastily, "do you secretly sympathize with them? After all, they *are* your countrymen."

"Don't be daft." Liam put as much disgust into his tone as possible to disguise the tremor he could not control.

"What made you go white then?"

"How should I be knowing?" He shrugged airily. "A goose walked over my grave." The expression, used often by his aunt, popped fortuitously into his head.

"Silly goose Rebecca walked over your grave?" Isaac's voice came mockingly from the doorway. He leapt nimbly off the veranda and tweaked his sister's long black braid. The dangerous question was forgotten as she raced after her brother, who danced tantalizingly just beyond her upraised hand.

A thought had been nagging at Liam ever since Isaac's return. Or perhaps Patrick's surprise visit had made him uneasy. During that two months of silence, he had forgotten the emotions that had drawn him to Patrick — anger at Gottlieb's short-tempered treatment, the longing for a family that was his by blood, the desire to be out and doing in the world. What had seemed like an adventure — no, be fair, a stand he should take for his father's sake — now looked like betrayal.

Isaac thinks it's a big joke, calling me a Fenian. But if he ever found out the truth, what would he say? A thought struck Liam so forcefully he had to sit down. Once they know, how can I stay here? I couldn't, he realized, with a sickening thud in his stomach. But where would I go? Patrick doesn't want me with him. The thoughts lodged blackly in his mind. How could he have been so stupid? Never once thought beyond the exciting job Patrick would have for him. Never imagined — an even worse thought — what the Fenians might do if they captured the peninsula. What would happen to people who got in their way — to Aunt Thirza, say, or Rebecca, or even Gottlieb — if soldiers fetched up here? And what about Isaac out on the battlefield?

A screech from Rebecca wrenched him out of his thoughts. "You beast!" she flung over her shoulder at her brother and stamped into the house, slamming the door after her. The reverberations shook the veranda right to the edge where Liam was sitting. He scrambled to his feet and found himself nose to nose with Isaac.

"What's up, bantling? Has that little cat been teasing?"

"Rebecca? No, it has nothing to do with Rebecca. I mean, there's nothing — nothing wrong."

"Then why are you looking as mournful as a ghost at a hanging?"

Liam shrugged and half-turned away. He couldn't bring himself to walk away, nor could he let Isaac's perceptive gaze rake his face. He knew only too well how easily his face gave away his thoughts. "Nothing's wrong," he said again, and even to his own ears he sounded pettish and sullen.

"Suit yourself." Isaac's heavy boots rang on the wooden veranda, the door slammed and Liam was alone.

Damnation, he thought, kicking at the gravel. The devil in Hell confound Patrick and all his works. What a dupe I've been. Believing that cock-and-bull story about oysters! The toe of his boot bit into the gravel again. I should have known the minute I picked it up. No smell. No sloshing. Didn't even have the right heft for oysters. But I've got to be sure. I'll check it…right now!

"Liam. Liam!"

Damn!

"You're wanted in the shop." Rebecca was standing in the doorway. When he hesitated,

half-turned, she added, "Right this minute."
He could hear satisfaction in every word.

Desperation urged him towards the stables.
Then sanity intervened. No sense in stirring
Rebecca's curiosity. No sense in antagonizing
Gottlieb. But he had to check on that cask —
soon!

CHAPTER

NINE

Kneeling in the dusty gloom of the horse stall, Liam rapped on the keg. A dull thud. He rocked it from side to side. No slosh. Fingers explored the smooth wood, the corded bands snugging the staves. It feels like an oyster keg. Hundreds were shipped from the Maritimes each month. They sat on counters in every hotel and tavern in Canada West. Why shouldn't this be one of them? He squinted, hoping to see stencilled letters that would reassure him. Too dark. One last try, he thought desperately. Crossing his fingers, he tapped again. Thunk! Face it — this is the stolen gunpowder!

Why does Patrick want it? His mind shied

away from the obvious conclusion. That afternoon as he sweated in the foundry, wondering — knowing really — what he would find in the stable, he had come to a decision. No matter what was in the keg, he wasn't hiding it any longer. He was going to get it off the Hahns' property as fast as he could.

The question was, how? He had slipped out of the house after supper. If the family had still been gathering around the table to share the light of the lamp, Liam would have been missed. But at this time of year, he should have an hour to himself. The immediate danger was from Rebecca and Aunt Thirza, who were taking advantage of the cool evening to plant beans in the kitchen garden. Still, if he left the stable by the back door he should be out of sight from the house.

So the next question was, where? I'd like to pitch you right in the canal. Get rid of you good and proper. Can I make it that far? Who might see me? He pictured the neighbourhood — farmers working their fields until last light, women sitting out on verandas doing the mending, travellers along the road perhaps. No, not the canal. Where, then? Just away from here! He scrambled to his feet, hoisting the keg under one arm, and made for the back door. It opened onto a hayfield that stretched to a long wood lot. Gottlieb had fenced the field to keep animals out but a path had been trodden through the hay for easy access to the woods. Liam glanced around. No one in sight!

He flitted across the dirt track behind the stable, slid the keg between the split rails and vaulted the fence. As he scooped it up again, he could see it was not the gaudy yellow of oyster kegs. *What does Patrick take me for, anyway?* He heard raised voices and dashed the last few yards.

Safe in the shelter of the woods, he sagged, panting, against a tree. The keg dragged at his left side but he didn't think of putting it down. Gulping a deep breath, he started through the wood lot, his footsteps making only muffled thuds on the forest floor. Small bushes and vines straggled along beside the path for twenty yards or so, but where the intertwining tops of the pines blocked the light, the forest floor was clear of underbrush. This late in the day it was hard to tell the black of the trees from the black of night. Liam felt safer and safer as he plunged into the forest. *Just a little farther,* he told himself, *and I can ditch it!*

He paused to take stock of where he was and for a moment thought he heard following footsteps. He stood still, listening, the cask nestled under his arm. Far above his head he could hear the swaying treetops. At foot level, rustling sounds whispered over the ground as small animals foraged. Nothing else.

Liam let his breath out slowly. Next problem — shall I just abandon this or try to hide it? Hide it where? No bushes, no holes. Doesn't matter! This is far enough. He set the keg on end and was about to leave when he heard a faint, melodic whistling. Liam's mind filled in the words, "When shall the swan, her death-note singing..." Patrick! Beads of sweat started under his arms and trickled down his sides. The whistling came closer. Liam could make out movement in the shadows and then an outline, taller than Patrick, broader than Patrick!

"Who are you?" Liam gasped.

"A friend."

Liam looked up past the bristly chin to black gaps where teeth had broken off, smelled breath foul from cheap whisky. He stepped back, nausea mixing with fear. "A friend of whom?" He could barely croak the words.

"A friend of our mutual friend." There was an Irish broadness in the vowels even though the voice had an edge like a file on rusty metal.

"I don't know who you mean."

"Do you not indeed, Liam O'Brien? I was told that tune would fetch you smart enough. Now, I'm a man of few words so let's be cutting the blather. I've come for that keg you've so obligingly fetched out here."

Thank God, Liam thought, relief flooding through him.

"And there's another little job for you."

Anger exploded in Liam. "Just who are you to be telling me there's a little job to do?" he demanded.

The man grabbed the front of his jacket in one huge hand, twisting the fabric so that his fist pushed Liam's chin up at an agonizing tilt. "Fergus Whelan, me fine boyo, that's who."

"Where's Patrick?" Liam whispered hoarsely, then swallowed and breathed deeply as the man loosened his jacket.

"Agh, away off on his travels. Saddled me with the rest of this." He looked sharply at Liam and suddenly barked, "And what might ye be doing here, any road? I reckoned on sitting in them woods half the night whistling like a damned bird to fetch you out. What is it you're up to, then?"

"Nothing." Liam swallowed a squeal as Fergus squeezed his arm. "I...I had to find a better place to hide the keg." Fergus released him. "But if you're going to take it," he babbled, "there's no problem."

"Take?" Fergus's lips twisted in what Liam supposed was a smile. "No, bucko, no. Exchange! We've a little trading to do." He seemed to consider for a moment. "And just how much would you be knowing about all this?"

"Not much. I know Patrick's a Fenian and…" His feelings of ill-use frothed like hops in beer "…and I know very well there's stolen gunpowder in that keg."

"You know that, do you? Well, blast Patrick for a loose-tongued, blethering…"

"He didn't tell me," Liam spit out scornfully. "I'm not that soft in the brain I couldn't figure it out."

"Agh, just as well you know. You'll be more careful of it."

"But you said you were taking it!"

"Exchanging it. 'Tis a little more work I've to do on this one."

"No!" Liam insisted, panic making him brave. "You'll have to take it. I can't… I can't…"

"Oh, but you can." Fergus grabbed Liam by his lapels again. "You've sworn an oath, haven't you? Unpleasant things have happened before now to them as tried to weasel out of that oath.

Understand?" On the last word he gave Liam a shake that rattled every tooth in his head.

"Y-yes," Liam hissed.

"Good!" Fergus unclasped his fist. "Listen carefully," the voice rasped. "We'll not be having any mix-ups. The kegs are full of gunpowder, right enough. These here are sealed tight with pinegum — and I've fixed detonators in the bung holes. Safe enough 'til I've fitted the primers. Then they'll go off when something hits them. Nice little gizmo."

Liam's scalp prickled. He loves this stuff. He's talking about blowing things up the way I'd talk about tomorrow's weather.

"Know anything about explosives, boyo?"

"No."

"No matter. When them kegs are needed someone'll tell you what to do. Here! Take a few of me fulminate primers separately. Safer that way." He reached into his coat pocket and produced a package about the size of a letter. It looked to Liam like oiled silk folded over and over into a square — a smaller version of the packet he had delivered to the ship chandler's! "Don't be getting these wet, and don't jiggle them about or you'll blow your hand off. Should be safe enough wrapped like that."

The voice calmly reeled off orders that made

Liam sweat with horror. Drops beaded under his hair and crawled like icy snails down his neck. What was Fergus going to blow up? The train? The canal? The town? He couldn't stand here listening. People he knew could be killed. But there in front of his eyes were Fergus's hairy fists, the huge knuckles. He forced himself to stand quietly, listening as the instructions went on and on.

"Heft that keg over here," Fergus said finally, beckoning Liam to follow. A few yards through the trees, near the edge of the wood lot, Fergus stopped. He whipped the keg from under Liam's arm and tucked it under his own, then tapped the toe of his boot on a dark shape under a tangle of vines and bushes. "These ones are ready. Mind you take good care of them. And don't you be forgetting, me bucko," he said jabbing Liam hard in the chest with a dirt-blackened index finger, "them as peaches, regrets it."

Liam stood numbly watching Fergus swing towards the path with his rolling sailor's gait. The second that Fergus was over the fence, panic took over and he was on his knees by the kegs. As he dragged one out of its nest of vines, he could feel something like a metal spigot in the bung hole.

A mine! My God, a mine! He remembered newspaper stories about the mines that had made the southern rivers so treacherous during the Civil War. But here — in a little place like Stonebridge?

Liam ran shaking fingers through his sweat-soaked hair. Where are you, Patrick? Why didn't you come? I have to explain to you…I've made a mistake. That night we met, I was angry, fed up. I didn't know what I was doing.

Crouching with his hands around the land-mine, Liam suddenly heard Patrick's voice as clearly as though he were standing before him: "Cursed be the hand and withered the arm that will not strike a blow for Ireland." Not my hand, Liam assured himself, gripping the keg even tighter. Patrick wouldn't curse my hands. It's just his flamboyant way of talking.

"Words count, Liam." Now it was his father's voice in his ears. "Don't use them carelessly. Make every word say what you mean."

Did Patrick mean every word?

"I don't care. I can't do it." Liam shoved the keg back under the bush and scrambled to his feet. He was out of the trees and several yards down the path when a thought stopped him. Fergus knows where they are. He can come back for them any time. I've got to move them.

He looked cautiously up and down the path and out across the field before hurrying back to the wood lot. When he reached Fergus's cache, he pulled both kegs out and rolled them along the forest floor to another set of bushes. He draped a vine over the place where twigs and branches had broken, then stepped back and gazed intently at the spot. "Now only I know where they are." Relief eased off the pain that had been squeezing his head. With luck the secret was safe again. Except — now he had mines, not just stolen gunpowder. He put his hand into his pocket and took out the package of oiled silk. Primers. Blow your hand off, Fergus said. What if — ? He looked up at the darkening sky. Time to get back. Shoving the packet deep into his pocket, he trudged out to the pathway and headed for the foundry.

CHAPTER

TEN

Swish. Thunk! Swish. Thunk! Swish. Thunk! Each time Liam's pickaxe bit into the earth, the shock travelled up his arm and jarred a grumbling tooth. He concentrated hard to fit into Isaac's rhythm. Thunk! and up. Thunk! and up. Like iron, this floor, he thought.

"For a bell weighing over two hundred pounds," Gottlieb had explained, as he marked out a four-foot square in front of the furnace, "we must the mould build where metal can pour directly into the sprue."

I'll never make it, Liam thought as he swung and swung and swung. He and Isaac had loosed off their right shoulder braces to allow for the full swing of their arms and tied handkerchiefs around their foreheads to catch the sweat. Halfway through the morning, when they shovelled the last of the loosened earth out of the hole, they had cleared barely twelve inches.

"…and three feet more to go," Liam groaned.

Isaac grinned at him. "Toughen your muscles, bantling." As they alternated rhythmic strokes, Liam found his thoughts nagging away at the same old problem. Forget about the casks, he told himself for the hundredth time in two days. Just forget the whole business. I've been no use to Patrick so far. Maybe he'll wash his hands of me. I'll stay close to the foundry. Patrick can't walk up to the door and ask for me, after all. I'll pretend it never happened. And the Hahns will never know. But there's Fergus. What if…?

"Time out for a bit, eh?" Isaac dropped his pick beside the hole they had quarried down another foot. Liam lowered his own pick and arched his back to unkink his shoulder muscles.

"Thirsty work." Isaac handed Liam a dipperful of water from the pail they had set near at hand. He reached for the second dipper.

Liam gazed over the lip of the dipper at Isaac's friendly, trusting grin. What if the Fenians do invade? And Isaac is on a train to the front? And Patrick and Fergus blow the train up? The water felt like ice in his stomach. No. It'll be all right. I've changed the hiding place. But I didn't move them very far. What if they stumble across them?

For two wakeful nights Liam wrestled with his problem. Will I? Won't I? What will happen to me if the Hahns find out? If I just forget about it? What if Fergus and Patrick have already come for the keg mines? Halfway through his second restless night, he threw off the covers and sat up. He was so drenched in sweat that the cool air made him shiver, and he hugged himself in silent misery.

The room was silver with moonlight reflecting off the white summer quilts. In the next bed Isaac snored softly. Isaac would never find himself in this kind of bind, Liam thought. No dithering for him. He didn't hesitate about volunteering when the Fenian scare first blew up. And in the foundry nothing fazes him. He can pour with a good steady hand, burnish with never a graze or a gouge and even stand up to Gottlieb. Well, at least, shrug off his tempers. No one stands up to Gottlieb.

But Isaac can certainly stand up to anyone else. Like the time Zeke Hansen had me by the throat up against a tree trunk, threatening to erase my freckles with a frozen road apple. Isaac sure made short work of him. "Here," Isaac had said, afterward. "Let me show you a few wrestling tricks. Can't have you backing down from the likes of Zeke Hansen." Well, wrestling tricks won't solve this little difficulty. Face it, Liam, you need help!

Liam looked again at the sleeping figure in the next bed. Yes, I'll tell him everything — right now. He leaned over, his hand outstretched to shake Isaac. No, I can't. Not fair. Gottlieb expects us both out at the clay pit at dawn. Besides, any noise might wake the others. He sat listening to the house sounds, little creaks and rustles from beds, the odd crack of drying wood, and over it all the steady buzz of Gottlieb snoring two rooms away. No. Even a whisper would carry in this house.

He huddled back under the covers and closed his eyes, but his mind refused to shut down. I can't wait. I must do something. He sat up suddenly and the bed springs squawked. He froze, glancing at Isaac, who rolled over, mumbled, then settled down again. What can I do? He scanned the room. His father's writing case stood on top of the bureau. Maybe a letter was the fastest way to tell the story.

Liam reached one foot to the floor, shifted his weight onto it, then crept across the room. The writing case, a wooden box with a sloped top, was compact — made for travelling. He carried it back to his bed, where the moonlight streaming in would catch the white of the paper. Easing himself down to keep the rope springs from creaking, he perched the box on his knees, slid out paper, pen and ink bottle, and began.

"Dear Isaac,

I've made a real mess of something and I need your help…"

As he scratched away, page after page, his burden seemed to lift slightly. Isaac always knew what to do about tricky problems. Perhaps there'd be time tomorrow — after dinner when Gottlieb had his nap. Enough time to cart those cursed kegs to the canal and dump them! Twelve hours from now, he thought, twelve hours and the problem will be solved. He sanded the wet ink on the last sentence, folded the letter, and tucked it into the writing case. First thing tomorrow, he vowed, as he set the box on the floor and curled back under the covers — he'd hand it to Isaac first thing, before they went downstairs.

But the next morning, when Liam finally struggled awake, Isaac's bed was empty. He jumped up and grabbed for his clothes. Dishes clattered downstairs. I've missed breakfast, he thought, struggling to pull up his trousers. Why did Isaac let me sleep? Oh, God, the letter! He snatched it from the writing case, jammed it into the frame of the mirror and bolted. Buttoning his trousers as he ran, he cleared the back stairs two at a time and headed for the pump in the yard. Shocked awake by the splash of cold water, he shrugged into his shirt, then headed across the yard to the foundry door. As he rounded the corner, his heart sank. The wagon, full of fresh wet clay, was backed up to the door. Too late to help with that.

From inside he could hear the slap, slap of wet clay hitting wood. Someone was working. He squeezed past the wagon and through the open doorway. In the grey light of the casting shed, he could see Isaac by a wooden trough near the big furnace. No Gottlieb, he realized with relief as he trotted across the space. Just then Isaac turned, his shovel ready for another load from the wagon.

"Well, well, Sleeping Beauty." The tone was light but Liam felt wary. No one took kindly to doing someone else's work.

"Sorry," Liam muttered. Reaching for a wooden hoe, he began stirring the clay that Isaac had shovelled into the trough. "Why didn't you wake me?"

"Tried," Isaac said over his shoulder. He drove the shovel into the clay, then said, "All I got were a few grunts for my pains. Not surprising. All that tossing and turning you do these nights. Don't feel so bright-eyed myself."

"Sorry," Liam said again. Tell him now, you dolt! The perfect time.

"All is ready?" Gottlieb strode out of the back room. Oh, the devil take him... Liam braced himself but Gottlieb merely frowned briefly in his direction. "Come, Isaac," he said. "Help me with this." He was carrying a large, flat board out of which had been cut the silhouette of half a bell. Gottlieb had announced at supper two nights ago that he was nearly ready to shape the core of the great bell. "So watch yourself," Isaac had warned Liam, "he's not going to be too even-tempered. The least thing off about this mould, and we'll have the bell cracking or sounding like a tin cow bell." Great, Liam thought, and I have to pick this morning to be late!

Gottlieb stood the wooden pattern against the furnace and then climbed down into the pit. It now had a plank floor on which he had built a framework of wood and wire in the shape of a cone. Isaac jumped down beside him. Each began scooping up handfuls of wet clay and patting them around the wooden cone. Liam stirred with the hoe. He'd been told the night before that he was to dribble water onto the clay as he stirred to keep it moist. Puddling, Gottlieb called it.

After an hour of concentrated work, Gottlieb straightened and stretched. Perfect, Liam thought, appraising the three-dimensional clay bell that now stood in the pit. Gottlieb walked around it frowning, then picked up his wooden pattern and fitted it at a ninety-degree angle against the smooth side of the clay bell. Gently he ran it around the shape to trim and smooth away the last unevenness. Halfway around the bell he stopped.

"Here we must build it up." He pointed to a shallow depression on the shoulder of the bell. He reached into the trough. "*Lieber Gott!*" he exploded.

Liam started out of his absorption. My God, the clay. Around the edges he could see a dry crust. "I'll fix it." He swung the hoe quickly and its sharp corner sliced across Gottlieb's knuckles. Blood welled up and dripped into the clay.

"Dummkopf!" Gottlieb roared, snatching his hand away.

"For God's sake, Liam," Isaac shouted at the same time. "Get out of here before you do some real damage."

Liam backed away as Isaac grabbed the hoe. "I'm sorry. I'm sorry. I..."

"Move!" Isaac ordered.

Liam trudged numbly out of the casting shed. You idiot, he groaned, you dithering idiot. He could hear the hoe scraping across the bottom of the trough and Gottlieb muttering about uneven drying. "You'll get nothing done with your head in the clouds," his father's voice sounded clearly in his ear. I know, Da. I know. Maybe it *is* my fault these things happen. And, he acknowledged almost with surprise, I really want to help with this bell. He jammed his hands into his pockets and scuffed his way through the gravel on the driveway. "But — first things first," his father's voice reminded him. "You have a problem to solve." Right, he thought gloomily. But how am I going to manage that? Isaac isn't too happy with me at the moment.

He wandered out into the back shed. A load of wood had been delivered and absent-mindedly he started to stack it. The rhythmic exercise and the steady thunk, thunk of wood on wood calmed him. Could I do it myself? he wondered. Carry two kegs as far as the canal? Too heavy. Roll them then? Too slow. Someone might see me. How then?

By dinner time, Liam was so hungry he could hardly think. But even though Aunt Thirza's thick soup comforted his stomach, the problem still churned through his mind. How?

"Pass the potatoes, please, Liam." Everyone at the table was staring at him.

"Are you feeling all right?" Aunt Thirza sounded concerned.

"Fine, thanks," Liam muttered, catching a quick glance from Isaac. No one had mentioned the morning's problems.

After dinner, Gottlieb headed for the parlour and his half-hour rest on the daybed. Rebecca and Thirza were busy tidying the kitchen. Isaac disappeared out the front door. Now's the time, Liam decided, wandering out to the veranda. But no plan. And no one to help.

With a flutter of panic, Liam paced the path that ran along the side of the house. He caught a glimpse of Rebecca, plate and dish towel in hand, peering through the kitchen window. Next thing I'll have her out here full of questions. Oh, forget Rebecca. How am I going to get the mines to the canal? A cart? No, I'd be seen. But... Throw the primers into the canal — or the rain barrel? Useless — Fergus has more. What, then?

His pacing brought him to the stable door. He leaned against it, staring at the tool rack on the wall. The hatchet! Of course. Split the kegs open, pour water over the powder and it's good-bye bombs. An hour at most and I'll be safe back. Then, for all I care, Fergus can whistle out here 'til his lips fall off.

Liam filled a bucket with water from the horse trough, snatched up the hatchet and marched off to the woods. Now that he had decided, he couldn't get it done fast enough. When he came to the clump of vines and ferns that covered the kegs, he threw himself on his knees and scrabbled at the undergrowth until one of the kegs lay uncovered, bung hole up. Now! He paused. What about the bomb mechanism wired into the hole? Would a blow from the hatchet...? Fergus said it needed a primer. Well, I guess I'm going to find out.

He took a deep breath, raised the hatchet over his head and brought it down with a satisfying whack. The keg cracked open, spilling powder into the ferns and pine needles. Now the second one! He swung the hatchet up.

Suddenly it was yanked backward out of his grasp. Something crashed on the back of his skull, and the world went black.

CHAPTER

ELEVEN

Liam blinked to clear his vision. The shards of light stabbing through a green haze hurt so much he had to squeeze his eyes shut again. Something sharp was digging into his shoulder blade. As he shifted slightly to get away from it, splinters of pain shot up the back of his neck and radiated from the base of his skull. He went limp again, swimming into darkness. The needles of pain were overlaid by voices, faint at first, then suddenly louder.

"Of course I had to stop him!" The harsh voice seemed to explode in Liam's ear. "You saw what he was up to." Fergus!

A softer voice seemed to disagree.

"Will ye stow your prattle, man. 'Tis all arranged. I strapped two of the bombs under the canal bridge early this morning. We set this one off at the railway tracks at eleven tonight and while everyone's rushing around out here, I light the fuse back at the bridge and it's goodbye canal. That's how a practical man works, my friend!"

The second voice demurred again. Even through the haze of pain, Liam recognized it — Patrick! Still too stunned to open his eyes, he strained to catch the words but only Fergus's disdainful jibes were audible.

"'Tis soft in the head you've gone since you met up with yon gossoon," he sneered. "Buck up, man. Wasn't it yourself said we're all tools for the Cause? What use is this one if he doesn't get his hands dirty?"

Again there was an indistinct but insistent protest.

"Face facts, man. Either he cuts the wires so we've a hold on him or we do away with him."

Wires? Liam's brain struggled to suppress the pain and make sense of the information. Rough hands seized him by the shoulders and the light behind his eyes flared, then blacked out.

He came around in a panic as sour bile

spewed from his mouth onto ground strewn with cinders. He blinked, trying to focus. In front of him a mound of earth rose steeply. The railway embankment, he realized, they've brought me to the tracks! He heard a thudding sound and turned his head cautiously, swallowing to keep the nausea at bay. Ten yards away dirt and gravel flew from a small-mouthed hole as Fergus and Patrick tunnelled into the side of the embankment. Then Fergus grabbed the bomb Liam had not been able to dismantle and stuffed it well back into the hole.

They're going to blow up the train tracks, Liam thought. I have to tell someone. He inhaled deeply, willing the dizziness to dissipate, then gathered his legs under him. Sprinting for the trees that lined the road, he heard Fergus shout. Faster, faster! Feet pounded after him and a sudden jerk at his shirt back sent him stumbling to his knees. A huge hand hauled him up again.

"Not so fast, boyo!"

Liam wrenched sideways. I've got to get free. I've got to... But the hand, twisted into the tough linen of his shirt, held him fast. He was dragged towards Patrick who stood, shovel in hand, beside the mined embankment. As he staggered to a halt, Liam gasped, "I must talk to you. You must understand…"

"I understand well enough what I saw." The hardness in the voice made Liam shiver. He wasn't like this back in the woods. He was sticking up for me. I'm sure he was. I'll make him understand.

"It was a mistake…I can't…I can't do anything that might harm the Hahns. Surely you can see my side of it? We're cousins, after all." The words tumbled out in breathless pants.

"Did you not swear a sacred oath, Liam O'Brien?"

"Yes, but…"

"Did you not swear, as every member of the glorious Brotherhood has sworn, to do your utmost, at every risk while life lasts?" Patrick's burning glare held Liam mesmerized. He had to blink to break the power.

"I cannot," he whispered. "My father…"

"Your father!" Liam flinched from the scornful tone. "A man who saved his own life at the cost of another's."

"No." Liam gasped. "That's not true. That's not the way it was."

"And for that treachery," Patrick continued inexorably, "for that treachery, Liam O'Brien, you owe the Cause one life."

"Stow it, the both of 'ee. 'Tis risky enough

doing this in daylight. Get him up that pole while I lay this fuse and fill the hole in."

Liam turned as Fergus grabbed the shovel from Patrick and strode to the embankment. Pole? he thought, remembering that barely heard conversation. Yes, they want the telegraph wires cut. He looked at the nearest pole, a rough-barked tree trunk with its branches carelessly lopped. No challenge — I could beat a squirrel to the top. He looked back at Patrick. "I won't," he said, bracing himself for an explosive reaction. But the hard glitter had died out of Patrick's eyes. He looked more the cousin Liam had met on the road to Chippewa.

"Now, Liam, wasn't it yourself begging me for an important job to do?" he murmured. "Well, here we are and you the only man of us light enough to shinny up that pole and cut the wires."

Liam set his chin and glared. Honey might get me once but not twice.

"For God's sake," Fergus exploded, throwing down the shovel as he strode back. Before Liam could react, he was grabbed by shirt collar and trousers and heaved up. "Grab on, damn you!" Liam instinctively threw his arms around the pole while his feet searched for toeholds.

147

"Now what did you go and do that for, and him with no clippers?" Patrick protested. "You'll be destroyin' us entirely with your impatience and temper."

For answer Fergus barked, "Here, you — catch" and Liam's right hand, almost by reflex, shot out and caught the clippers. He searched with a toe, found another branch stub and hitched himself further up the pole. When he was level with the cross-arms where wires had been strung on blue glass knobs, he stopped. Make a grab for me now, he thought, looking at Fergus from his six-foot advantage, and you'll get a head full of boot.

"Cut them, damn you!" Fergus snarled as Liam scanned the countryside. Suddenly he caught a flicker of movement through the trees, then another. Isaac!

Patrick was several feet from the pole. Fergus stood right under it, glaring up. Keep their eyes on me, Liam prayed and reached slowly with the clippers towards a wire. Deliberately he looked away from Isaac, who was silently covering the ground between the line of trees and the tracks. Suddenly he heard a grunt of surprise. Isaac had grabbed Patrick from behind in a wrestling hold. Fergus whirled, raising his shovel. Liam dropped backward off the pole, crashing on top of Fergus. Dazed from the impact, Liam rolled to his knees while Fergus lay gasping for breath. Thank God, Liam thought as he struggled to his feet and snatched up the shovel. Thank God for Isaac!

Isaac had grabbed Patrick from behind, arms up under his shoulders and hands locked behind his neck. Liam knew it was a hard hold to break but Patrick was twisting out of it with surprising swiftness. A heel to Isaac's instep and he was free. His right hand sliced sideways and up.

"Watch out!" Liam shouted as Isaac jumped back.

"Freeze, gents!" Alf Wister, his feet planted firmly apart, trained two pistols on the combatants. Patrick's hands dropped to his sides as the junkman gestured with one pistol. "Stand clear, boys. I like to make sure I got the right pistol pointed at the right gizzard. That's right, you come on over here by me."

Where did he come from? Liam stumbled behind Isaac until they both stood clear of the pistols. Fergus was pulling himself slowly to his feet, gasping for breath. Alf eyed him warily.

"Now don't ask me to display my marksmanship, gents. Just believe I've never missed yet." He nodded at Liam. "My wagon's back down the road apiece. Fetch that rope I've left handy on the seat. I reckon this interesting bit of scrap'll need to be well tied down." Liam was halfway to the road before Alf had finished laughing at his own joke.

"Hands behind your backs, gents," Alf was ordering as Liam returned. "Now, young sirs, a few tight loops around them wrists."

Isaac grabbed a length of rope and headed for Fergus. Liam looked at the rope in his hands and then at Patrick, who stood ramrod straight facing Alf. Hesitantly he came up behind his cousin and slipped a loop around the wrists, flinching as flesh touched flesh.

"Right," Alf said, standing out of arm's reach at the ready while Liam and Isaac worked, "time to be off."

Off where? Liam wondered. To jail? And what's going to happen to me? He pulled the last knot tight, then flicked a glance to where Isaac had just finished pinioning a loudly cursing Fergus. Isaac looked past Liam to the junkman. "I want to know who you are."

The little man raised one fuzzy eyebrow and grinned. "Why, Alfred J. Wister, young sir, dealer in scrap metals." He twirled one pistol, then jammed it into the waistband of his baggy trousers. The other he uncocked but held loosely in his right hand.

"Don't give me that! You didn't just turn up here by chance. You've been snooping about for months. Are you army?"

"Now do I look like army?" Alf picked idly at a spot of soup crusted on his threadbare waistcoat. "You think as high as you can think. That's where I gets me orders."

"Government?"

"Let's just say I'm a ferret for them as needs eyes where they ain't got eyes."

Liam shivered. A spy for the government!

"Time to move out. Hoist up that there keg, young master. That's Crown evidence. Forrard march, gents." Alf dug the pistol into Fergus's ribs and urged him towards the wagon, which was just barely visible down the line of trees.

Isaac had the cask of gunpowder under one arm and was striding on ahead, leaving Liam to straggle behind. What will Isaac think about this, he worried. How can I explain about Patrick? He's not just a ruffian like Fergus. There's something about him... He looked at the figure marching in front of him. Not defiant like Fergus, almost — Liam struggled to find the right word — almost triumphant. And again that eerie melody rippled through Liam. "When shall the swan, her death-note singing, sleep, with wings in darkness furled." Darkness. Is that what it is about Patrick — a darkness in him? How can I possibly explain that?

Alf had left the tailgate of the wagon down. It was sturdy enough to make a ramp for hauling heavy scrap into the wagon and now he was prodding the prisoners towards it. Suddenly Fergus kicked backwards, caught Alf hard in the shins, then dodged sideways. But Isaac was too quick for him. He grabbed one pinioned arm and Alf, small but wiry, grabbed the other side. Together they wrestled Fergus onto the wagon.

As the commotion started, Liam found Patrick staring straight at him. He could make out neither pleading nor condemnation on Patrick's face. He wanted to say something. Instead, he was behind Patrick, picking frantically at the clumsy knots. As the ropes fell away, Patrick leaped like a hare into the trees without a word or a look for Liam.

Alf snatched out his pistol and fired. Patrick staggered. "Got him!" — but it was a momentary pause only. He was running again.

"I'll catch him," Isaac shouted, leaping from the wagon.

"Let him go." Alf stooped to pick up the discarded rope. Liam braced himself for angry questions but Alf just said, "I've got the one I want. This one's the brains. That one's small potatoes."

Patrick? Small potatoes? The junkman's voice rambled on as though he were thinking out loud. "Pretty poor job of knot making. Seems to have untied itself real easy. Well, you want a thing done proper, do it yourself, I reckon." As he spoke, he coiled the rope round and round the length of his right arm from hand to elbow.

Liam cleared his throat, swallowing what seemed like a mouthful of cobwebs. "There's something you should know..." he started.

The junkman cocked an interrogative eyebrow at him.

"Fergus knocked me unconscious," Liam began. God, don't start with that. Don't make excuses! "But I came 'round," he hurried on, "in time to hear them talking about two bombs Fergus'd tied underneath the bridge over the canal. Fergus was going to light the fuses around eleven tonight. I don't know if anyone else was in on this or knew about the bombs...or anything," he ended lamely.

"Right!" Alf tossed the loop of rope into the wagon beside a well-trussed Fergus. "I'll see to it — don't you fret yourself." He shot the bolts on the wagon gate. "A word to the wise, young sirs," he said over his shoulder as he strolled to the front of the wagon. "Things is startin'. You'd best get back on home. There'll be an important message coming through them wires what didn't get cut." Then he heaved himself up onto the high front seat and clucked to his horses.

As the wagon rumbled down the road with its writhing, cursing bundle firmly tied to the side supports, Isaac turned on Liam.

"What the blue-blazing hell do you think you've been doing?"

CHAPTER

TWELVE

How can I say I've been stupid, that I'm sorry? Will Isaac believe me? Will anyone? Liam stared at the toes of his boots.

"Well?" Isaac prompted.

"Does... does your father know about any of this?"

"No. And I don't want him to know anything."

"What?"

"I don't want him hurt," Isaac said firmly. "How do you think he's going to feel when he hears that someone he's given a home to — trained in his craft! — has been mixed up with people like that?"

Liam's thoughts went scrambling after this new idea. "I never…"

"You never thought! You act as though you're the only one with feelings."

"Feelings!" The pent-up resentment and anger of the past months swept through Liam. "What does he care about my feelings? All he does is shout and bully. Everything I do is wrong…" His voice shook. Stop, he told himself, before you disgrace yourself.

After a minute Isaac said quietly, "I know he has a short temper. I've been on the receiving end often enough."

"You! You do everything right." Why did that have to sound petulant?

"I didn't. I had to learn, too, you know. And he didn't have much patience while I was learning."

Isaac shouted at, made to feel clumsy and useless? And still loving such a father?

"He does it because he cares so much about the craft," Isaac continued. "He wants everything that comes out of his shop to be perfect but that doesn't mean he doesn't care about people. And I won't have him hurt by you." They had been walking down the road towards the foundry but Isaac stopped. "I mean that, Liam. I won't let you hurt him. Nothing's come of this fiasco so he doesn't need to know. All we have to do is think of a good reason for being away from the foundry. So, think!"

Relief made Liam weak at the knees. No one will know. No one will know! But — Da, what do you think? Is it the coward's way out? He walked along silently, studying the ground. Tell me, Da, what should I do?

"Come on, Liam, think. We'll be there soon."

"I…I think I ought to tell him."

"What! Just walk in there and announce to the assembled household that you've been spying for the Fenians?"

"Yes." Liam squared his shoulders and looked Isaac straight in the eyes. "That's exactly what I'm going to do."

"And what do you think my father will do?"

Liam winced. It wasn't only cast bronze that Gottlieb Hahn expected to be perfect.

Liam rallied his courage. "He may turn me in for — for conspiracy — and I guess I'd have to leave the foundry."

"Exactly — and you'd break his heart." Isaac's sharp reply shook Liam. "Tell me everything," Isaac demanded. "I can't help unless I know what's been going on."

Liam hesitated. Do I want help? Complete confession — wasn't that the only way?

"Who were those men?" Isaac prompted. "The one who got away, who was he?"

"My cousin, Patrick Danaghy."

"And the other one?"

"A ruffian, a thug!" Liam spat the words out. Fergus! All his fault! "They were both soldiers in the Union Army. Now they're Fenians." Pain was pounding through his bruised head. "I can't remember everything Patrick said about the Cause." Why had it made so much sense when Patrick explained it?

"What were you supposed to do?"

"Nothing wonderful. Act as lookout mainly. Meet Patrick. Report what I saw."

"So that's what Rebecca meant."

"Rebecca?"

"She saw you up in the cupola. Behaving strangely, she said. Saw you out in the stables hiding something, too."

Rebecca again!

"You needn't look like that." Isaac's voice sharpened. "Lucky for you Rebecca can put two and two together and make some sense of it. She sent me after you."

"How did she know?"

"Found the letter when she was dusting. Yes, she can be a pest — sticking her nose in and giving opinions that aren't wanted. But God

158

knows where you'd be right now without Rebecca. Old Alf sure wouldn't have known where to find you."

"What are you talking about? Where did Alf Wister come from anyway?"

"Showed up at the house just after dinner. Wanted to talk to Father in his office. I didn't have time to be curious because Rebecca shoved me upstairs. Why on earth leave that note in the bedroom? How was I supposed to find it there in the middle of the day?"

Liam flushed and shrugged sheepishly.

"The way you've been acting lately..." Isaac sounded defensive. "I was all set to throw it in the fire, but Rebecca grabbed it. Father called: Alf Wister wanted to question us. Who knows what he said to make Father co-operate?" Isaac rolled his eyes. "Explained he was on the look-out for Fenians and had we seen anything being so near the railway line and the canal. Well, with your note... and Rebecca glaring at me, I didn't know where to look. Finally old Alf heads out and just as he's climbing onto his wagon, Rebecca goes haring after him, hissing at me to follow and tell him about your note. Before I know what's happening, I'm up beside him and we're off to rescue you."

"Didn't you ask him what he was up to?"

"Yeah, I asked. All I got was 'Them as needs to know, knows, young master.'" Isaac leered and mugged in imitation of Alf, his high spirits bubbling again. "Obviously he's a government agent, but…a scrap dealer? A junkman! Would the government really use a junkman?"

At the front gate Isaac turned to Liam. "Well?"

Liam hesitated. Make up some story? Yes or no? Or tell the plain truth and take whatever comes? Before he could decide, the door flew open. "The Fenians are coming," Rebecca cried. "The militia's been called out!"

The boys looked at each other. "Leave it," Isaac ordered. "You can't say anything now." He wheeled and ran towards Rebecca. "How do you know?" he demanded.

"Mr. Hansen — on his way back from town." Her eyes met Liam's. Was that reproach? How can I possibly say nothing when she knows?

"Isaac, have you heard?" Aunt Thirza came through from the kitchen. "The militia is to assemble by eight tonight."

"Right, I'm off to pack." He took the stairs two at a time. "Liam, come and help me."

"Yes, Liam, go." Aunt Thirza pushed him towards the stairs. "Rebecca, Isaac must have supper before he goes."

"Just one minute, Aunt, please." Rebecca tore after Liam, not waiting for an answer.

"Tell me!" she hissed when all three were in the back bedroom. "Every detail. Exactly what happened."

"It was nothing. Believe me it was nothing..." Liam began ruefully.

"Oh, I don't know," Isaac objected. "Jumping off that pole onto Fergus was pretty good."

Liam shrugged.

"And how about old Alf?" Isaac dropped his voice an octave, pointed a finger and growled, "Freeze, gents."

"Tell me," Rebecca pleaded, "tell me!"

"No time. Have to get ready," Isaac teased. "Old Liam here'll tell you everything later. But — how come no explosion when we got back?"

"Papa didn't know you were out. First thing after Mr. Wister left, he called Aunt Thirza into the office."

"I don't suppose you were able to hear anything."

"A little."

"Well?"

"You'll never believe this."

Isaac had been flinging clothes out of the tall wardrobe as they talked. "Never mind the dramatics. Just give," he ordered. Liam, scrambling under the bed for boots, stuck his head out to listen.

"Well," she began, "after I sent you off with Mr. Wister…" Isaac pulled his head out of the wardrobe and glared. She started again. "Their voices were very low so…"

"Just tell it straight." Isaac tossed his haversack to Liam, who began packing socks and shirts into it.

"All right then," Rebecca said huffily. "Alf Wister is a government agent. What do you think of that!"

Isaac gave a disgusted grunt. "Is that all? We figured that out for ourselves!"

Rebecca's face fell. "How?"

"Liam will tell you. What else?"

"The Queen's Own Rifles are arriving tomorrow noon from Toronto."

"Good. Anything else?"

"Rebecca!" Aunt Thirza's call came up the stairs.

"Coming!" Rebecca jumped off the bed.

"Wait a minute!" Isaac grabbed hold of his sister as she dashed past. "No word of this to Father or Aunt Thirza, understand?"

Rebecca looked at Liam, who felt his face go red, then back at her brother. "Aunt Thirza

162

hasn't said anything but I'm sure she saw you riding off on the wagon."

"Probably thought I just wanted to talk to old Alf."

"Women aren't stupid, Isaac," Rebecca said tartly.

"Meaning?"

"She probably suspected as soon as I did that Liam was up to something."

"I'm going to tell them," Liam said stiffly.

"Don't be selfish," Isaac said sharply. "They have enough to worry about. You'll just have to sweat it out. And, Rebecca, not a word from you either."

"Rebecca!" The call was sharper.

"I wish I'd been there," Rebecca said to Liam. "Together we could have fixed those two."

Liam grinned weakly. "Um…" He took a deep breath. He had a debt to pay. "Thank you for … for finding the letter and … everything."

Something about Rebecca's embarrassed nod made Liam feel warm.

CHAPTER

THIRTEEN

Two days. Liam hunched himself into the corner of the cupola. Still no news.

Go look 'round the countryside, Gottlieb had said. What's the use? Battle's too far east. Nothing in town but trains unloading soldiers.

He cradled his father's spyglass across his knees and laid his head against the bell. Two days! How much longer could he avoid the questions in Aunt Thirza's eyes, swallow another mouthful of Gottlieb's food? The cool metal eased the pain. He turned and put his forehead on it, relaxed against it, closed his eyes — and the dream started again. Two figures, locked chest to chest, swaying back and forth, spinning. As they turned he could see

164

Patrick grinning at him, then Isaac, clench-jawed and frowning. A never-ending fight, every time he closed his eyes.

He sat up again and ran his hand around the sound bow, making the bell murmur. Think about her songs, he told himself. Forget everything else. He heard again the furious alarm clamoured to the countryside as the militia gathered in Port Colborne. And yesterday the slow, deep tolling for the dead after the telegraph message about the battle lost at Ridgeway. Rebecca had cried for joy because Isaac wasn't at Ridgeway but the figures in Liam's nightmare now had guns.

He closed his eyes and saw the first time Isaac had handed him a gun. "Every man should be able to fill his own larder," Isaac had decreed, after Liam explained that in Ireland only the gentry were allowed to go out after pigeons or hares. What a dummy I must have looked, Liam thought, remembering all the missed shots — but the truth was he hated that moment when the pigeon tumbled in midflight or the rabbit lurched...like Patrick, stumbling as the bullet hit. Where is he? With the invaders? Spying out the land? Wounded? I don't care! He tricked me, lied to me. I will *not* think of Patrick.

Back to business, he decided, focusing the spyglass on the railway tracks to the east. Just visible in the distance was a puff of white smoke. The dead, he thought, from Ridgeway. Yesterday the same train had rumbled past with the wounded.

Where are you, Isaac?

Gottlieb had discovered that Isaac's artillery unit was being shipped to Fort Erie by steamer. Liam tried to picture that trip — so pleasant on an ordinary day — along the lake shore and into the Niagara River. A bustling little port Fort Erie was the day he'd seen it with Da. But now? Somewhere near there, rumours said, the Fenians had crossed the river. Please, please be safe, Isaac!

He tried to peer beyond the tiny train but all was fuzzy greens and blues. He swung his spyglass to the right. A wagon. Mr. Hansen? News from town? As it rumbled closer, he could see something dark tumbled in the back. He twisted the eyepiece. The bundle moved. Sun glinted off brass buttons. Oh, God! Oh, God! Isaac? Liam scrambled for the trapdoor. As he clattered down the stairs he heard himself panting, Please, please, please...!

He was halfway down the last flight when the kitchen door crashed open and Rebecca came flying out. "Wagon coming," she cried, dashing for the front gate.

"Wait," Liam called. What if it was Isaac — wounded? She shouldn't see… "Wait, Rebecca!" But she was already out the gate and waving for the wagon to stop.

As Liam ran up beside her, Mr. Hansen said, "Got something for yuh." Rebecca shrieked, "Isaac!" and Liam had to grab for the side of the wagon as his knees went weak. He's home!

"Liam, come help!" Rebecca cried, as Isaac swung himself stiffly over the tailgate of the wagon.

"Where are you hurt?" Liam ducked under Isaac's arm and propped him from one side while Rebecca did the same for the other side.

"Not wounded," Isaac groaned. "Everything aches. Tell you later." The hand draped over Liam's shoulder was streaked black with gunpowder and blood. Mud had dried in white splotches on the navy uniform, which reeked of cordite and sweat.

As they lurched up the steps, the door flew open. "Sit him down here," Thirza said, pulling forward the kitchen rocker. "Some cider, Rebecca! He must be parched."

As Isaac collapsed into the rocker, Liam searched the face smeared black with gunpowder. I was so afraid for you, Isaac, he wanted to say. Tears stung his eyes. He turned away to hide them and saw Gottlieb sitting ramrod straight, eyes riveted on Isaac. Liam barely heard the murmured, "*Gott sei dank. The Lord be praised.*"

With a strained rasp Gottlieb said, "Tell us, my son."

Isaac gulped greedily at the ale Rebecca handed him. "I'll be telling you for years. There's so much…"

"Let the boy eat," Thirza admonished. But before Isaac had swallowed two mouthfuls of the cold meat and buttered bread, she was back with a damp cloth to wipe his face. "You look like you've been dragged through a hedgerow backwards," she scolded lovingly.

Finally Isaac pushed his plate away and sat with his head back, eyes closed, breathing deeply.

"Tell us," Rebecca beseeched.

Isaac opened his eyes. "I have leave until first light tomorrow," he announced.

"And you must sleep for most of it," Thirza ordered as Rebecca exclaimed, "You mean you have to go back?" and Liam protested, "But they have five thousand soldiers now!"

"Tell us just a little." Gottlieb's voice trembled,

almost pleading. Liam saw him swallow before he could add, "We were worried…"

"We were so afraid you were wounded or…" Rebecca added.

"What happened that you were so long?" Thirza prompted.

Isaac shifted and stretched in the hardbacked chair. "Well, you knew we'd gone round to the Niagara by tug? We were cruising the shoreline looking for action. Just reached the wharf at Fort Erie when a couple of scouts came galloping up shouting, 'Fenians coming!' No sooner ashore than we saw them — snaking through the town in skirmishing formation. Everywhere we turned another one popped out from behind a building or up from behind someone's rain barrel. We spread out, no sense making a sitting duck target. About twenty of us holed up in an empty house taking potshots at any head that showed itself. Kept up a pretty smart round of firing. No one broke through to get into the house, but my ammunition was getting low. Saw Bill Brown and Jim Boyle fixing bayonets. That meant they were already out.

"Then we heard shouting from outside — cursing really." Isaac grinned at his aunt.

"Go on. Go on," Rebecca urged.

"We fired another round. 'Burn 'em out,' we

heard. Then smoke started to curl up past the front window. 'Out the back!' Bill shouted, but every window showed Fenians with fixed bayonets. So…" Isaac shrugged, "nothing to do but surrender."

He's ashamed, Liam thought, watching Isaac's sinewy hands ball into fists. He pictured himself in that house at Isaac's side facing… Patrick?

"And then?" Gottlieb prompted.

"…choking on the smoke, so — no choice. Had to file out the door and throw our guns down. A gang of them rushed us — real cutthroats they were. Ready to shoot us where we stood. Then General O'Neill came striding up threatening to shoot any man who touched a prisoner."

Gottlieb nodded. "An army man, so the papers say. An officer on the Union side. He would respect the rules of war."

"Calmed 'em down, anyway. We were soon trussed up. Pretty boring, after that. Just wait, wait, wait. At midnight — I'd actually dozed off! — our guards started prodding us to our feet. Couldn't figure what was happening. Then we were stumbling along in the dark, hands still tied. Next thing, we're at the wharf. Saw Fenians swarming aboard a raft. Jake, next to me, said, 'Guard's taken off! Let's go.' Well, easier said than done. Best we could do was huddle together and let men—dozens it seemed like — push past us. Finally we stumbled into the corner of a building and managed to untie each other.

"Sky brightening. Place nearly deserted. Could see men scrambling out into the water, some in rowboats, dozens with nothing but barrel staves or broken boards to hold onto, trying to float across — bobbing about like corks, they were. We were too hungry to care! Straggled back into Fort Erie and found a kitchen with some stale bread and cheese. Then, damned if there wasn't another invasion!"

"Oh, no!" Rebecca's hand flew to her mouth but Isaac was laughing.

"*Our* forces had finally arrived. Hundreds of them — flags flying, bugles blowing...and hardly a Fenian in sight!"

"You mean there were still *some?*"

"Oh, yes. Scouts and pickets hadn't been called in. Nasty surprise they had in store." Isaac yawned until the hinges of his jaws cracked, then rubbed his eyes. "That's about all. We were sent back on the tug and told to report in by dawn tomorrow."

"But why?" Rebecca demanded. "It's all over. You defeated them. There's nothing left to do."

"Sent that lot packing. But there are thousands of them! I saw masses across the river. Guess they've got just as many in Chicago. And another bunch somewhere along the St. Lawrence. We've only just begun." He yawned hugely again, and Aunt Thirza stood up.

"That's enough!" she said. "This boy has to get some sleep. Liam, go up with him. Then bring me down his uniform. Rebecca, see if the water is hot enough for washing. Up you go, Isaac," she said, hustling her nephew towards the stairs.

"...sorry...t'be such a...damper on th' party, Liam..." Isaac stumbled the last few steps and fell across the bed. Fast asleep, Liam realized, as he stripped off the muddy uniform. Thank God you're home, he whispered. Thank God you're home. He tugged the last sock off, then pulled a light cotton quilt over the spread-eagled form before tiptoeing downstairs with the grubby bundle.

Thirza whisked the uniform from his hands and took it out on the veranda for a stiff brushing. Rebecca had a tub set up at the foot of the steps into which she plunged all the under clothes. Liam prowled the yard, his nerves twitching. Was Patrick floating across the river on a raft of barrel staves? The picture didn't square with what he knew of Patrick. But...

He kicked at the firewood piled along the wall of the barn. I have to do something, he thought, plunging off in the direction of the road. Behind him he heard the screech of the pump handle — Rebecca working off her nervous energy on the washing! He started to run, thudding steadily along the hard-packed road until he could feel nothing but the blood pulsing through his veins, then reeled off the road towards a tree. As he leaned panting against the rough bark, a familiar melody floated into the silence. "When will heaven, its sweet bell ringing, Call my spirit..." It couldn't be...It couldn't be! The mournful whistling grew louder. Hobbling towards him, through the trees, was a familiar figure.

What will I say? How can I face him? Then "Fool!" he said fiercely, as he realized that part of what he felt was shame. For letting Patrick down? Fool!

"Well met, cousin." The soft voice sent shivers through Liam. He managed only a nod. The man standing before him was no longer the bright, devil-may-care wanderer he had met three months earlier. The spring had gone from his step, he stumbled on the uneven ground, and one arm was folded in a sling across his chest.

"A memento of our last meeting," he said, noticing Liam's glance. "And if that long face on you is pity for me arm, think nothing of it. The ball broke the bone, but it's mending. Played old Harry with me plans for a certain affair I was to attend, though."

"You weren't part of the invasion?" Liam had to force the words out.

"That I was not."

Relief swept through Liam. Why should it matter that Patrick didn't take part in the fighting? "Where were you?" he barked.

"Around and about! 'Tis scarcely the healthiest neighbourhood for a man with the sound of Ireland on his tongue, but I managed." He glanced sideways at Liam out of those green cat's eyes. "I'll be away out of the country by midnight tonight, but I found I couldn't take myself off with this unfinished business between us."

"What business?'

"Shall we sit awhile?" Patrick nodded to the grassy verge. "'Tis pleasanter for talking."

Liam lowered himself warily onto the grass, glanced both ways along the deserted road, then flushed when he caught Patrick's sardonic eye on him.

Patrick folded himself down awkwardly, one-handed, to sit with his back against a stout tree. "Well, cousin," he nodded towards the sling when they were both settled. "'Twould seem I owe you a word of thanks for me freedom — perhaps even for me life?"

Liam nodded curtly, unwilling to trust the honey of that voice. Risking his life in a hostile country for a mere word of thanks? Unlikely!

"And you'll be asking why else am I here?"

Liam flushed. My face, giving me away again!

"There's a question needs an answer."

Liam eyed his cousin uneasily. "If you mean changing my mind about helping you…"

"Helping me, is it? You were a sworn soldier in a sacred Cause."

Oh no, you don't get me that way! "And is Fergus Whelan a sworn soldier in that Cause?"

"He is."

"That thug thinks no more of Ireland and her oppression than… than…"

"Ah, cousin! — and doesn't every cause use the tools needed to do the job?"

"At least it's him in jail and not you. That's why I untied you. The thought of you going to jail with that murdering…"

"Wirra, Liam! D'ye still not understand? Had my work been done, I'd have welcomed jail. Where but from jail can a man protest the state of things? From jail! The very symbol of British oppression."

"You broke the law! You were trying to kill people who never did a thing to hurt you!"

"Who would see misery and injustice if they could look the other way? We have to make them turn and face it."

"You're talking about people who've never seen Ireland. People whose food and friendship I've accepted. People I care about!"

"Liam, Liam! There's no room for personal feelings in a righteous Cause! At this very moment thousands in Ireland have no food in their bellies."

"There's nothing I can do, here in Canada, about that," Liam insisted — his own voice flat, tight as he fought against the power of Patrick's spell.

"Can ye not?" Those glittering eyes held Liam's again. "There was a time you thought differently, Liam O'Brien. A time you swore a sacred oath. An oath you have now foresworn."

"Yes, I've been thinking about that." Liam took a deep breath and plunged in, his words already planned. "That oath said 'all things not contrary to the laws of God.' What you were planning was murder."

"Ah! Hair-splitting is it? And just when did you become a lawyer? What you did was treachery plain and simple — and in Ireland, you'll remember, we've a short way with traitors."

Liam leaped to his feet and was backing away when Patrick's brittle laugh stopped him. "Of what danger to you is a one-armed man?" he mocked. "Come, cousin, help me up." He reached with his free hand and Liam, choking with rage and mortification, pulled him to his feet.

"So, 'tis farewell, cousin," Patrick announced coolly. "It's me for Ireland at the end of the month. Word's out the Young Irelanders are active again."

"Why must you go looking for danger? What good can this do? Why not stay here?" Liam said impulsively, surprising himself. "Make a new life!"

"A new life? Ah, Liam, Liam, will ye never understand? As long as one Irish woman sleeps in a hovel, or one Irish child cries for bread, or one English agent lords it over an honest Irish farmer, there will be no peace, no new life for any Irishman worthy of the name."

"My father said…"

"Your father! A man who fled the Cause! The names to call on, as you well know, are Wolfe Tone and Daniel O'Connell. In the name of those glorious martyrs, we will prevail." Patrick's eyes shone, focused, not on Liam, but on some distant vision only he could see.

A deep melancholy swept over Liam. He wants to die. He is yearning to die a martyr's death just like Wolfe Tone and Daniel O'Connell and the whole parade of them back to Fionnuala herself. And then Liam realized that the "sweet" bell in the old song called its listeners to death. That's what he had never understood — it offered only death, no hope. That's why his father had never liked it.

He faced his cousin. "We're too different, Patrick. Your road is not my road."

Patrick's eyes lost their faraway stare. "Is it not, wisha? More fool me then, to have hoped. 'Tis just as well, perhaps. Attachments distract. Walk with me to the crossroads yonder, cousin. From there it is *slan leat*, our final farewell. I shall not return from Ireland."

Liam shuddered. "No, Patrick, not even as far as the crossroads." He turned on his heel and walked briskly for perhaps a hundred heartbeats. Then his steps faltered. This is wrong. I must at least say good-bye.

178

He turned. No one. Patrick might never have been there. Liam sighed. "*Slan leat*, cousin," he whispered, and turned his face firmly towards home.

CHAPTER

FOURTEEN

The sun beating down made his head swim. Need food. At dinner he'd pushed aside the cold meat and bread. Then Isaac had come and now Patrick... Did I mean what I told Patrick? What's Ireland to me? Da said, start a new life. If he thought this was right... Yes, I do want to. I'll try harder, just like Da told me and...

A sour, sick taste backed up into his throat. But what about them? Will they let me stay? Will they want me...after what might have happened to Isaac? He trudged on, and with each step a pain like a tiny hammer struck hard at his temples. He rubbed the spots with his forefingers. How can the Hahns ever forgive me? Well...I guess if they won't, they won't. But... He took a deep breath and squeezed his eyes shut. I know, Da, I know — I have to tell them.

He turned in at the pathway to the house and eased the gate open. Would Gottlieb be back out in the foundry or...? He inched the kitchen door open. Thirza was alone — resting in the rocking chair by the window, eyes closed. Liam hesitated on the threshold.

"It's all right, Liam. I'm awake."

He cleared his throat nervously. "I have something to tell you," he said. "All of you."

She looked intently at him, then nodded. "Good. I'm very glad. Come. My brother is in the parlour."

Gottlieb was sitting on the end of the settee rubbing his hands over his face to shake off sleep. He looked up questioningly.

Liam took a deep breath to steady his voice. "I have something I must tell you, sir."

Gottlieb looked from boy to woman. "It is important, brother, that you listen carefully to the whole story."

"So," Gottlieb said finally. "Come. We will sit at the table."

As Liam sat tensely in his usual place, he saw Rebecca creep in and huddle onto the chair beside her aunt. Only Isaac's place was empty.

"We are listening," Gottlieb said. "Speak."

Liam's throat went dry. *Where will I start?* Pictures flashed through his mind... the foundry... those misshapen bells. *I was feeling hurt and fed up so...*

He cleared his throat. "I...I guess it started about three months ago — my cousin Patrick Danaghy came walking out of a dark night and... and heaven knows, I wish he'd never..." He choked, cleared his throat again then, caught up in the details, spoke steadily.

The part about delivering the package to the ship chandler's and meeting Alf Wister went well enough. All those trips up the cupola scanning the countryside were nothing interesting. But when he came to the part about the mines made out of kegs, his voice faltered. He had hoped, when he told this story, to sound heroic, a warrior going into battle — instead he sounded like a dupe, a pawn in the hands of unscrupulous men. And when he came to the part about being terrorized by Fergus, he sounded like a coward. His voice sank almost to a whisper as he told how he had hidden the casks mostly because he was afraid of what Fergus might do to him. He stopped at the point where he ran away from Fergus, too tired to go on.

"And so?" Gottlieb's voice prodded him.

"I had decided…" Liam paused to lick his dry lips "…that the bombs had to be destroyed."

"This part is of great interest. Continue."

"I couldn't think how. Then I thought — water. I was going to ask Isaac to help but that morning things were so…" He let the sentence drift into silence. "I felt… it's hard to explain… just that I had to do something about them fast. I took the hatchet to split the kegs open. Fergus caught me at it and knocked me out." Involuntarily Liam reached up to feel the still tender bruise.

"Continue."

"There's not much else. When I came 'round I was by the railway tracks. Fergus and Patrick were planting the mine. They tried to get me to cut the telegraph wires. Snarling me up in their schemes, so I'd be afraid to tell on them," Liam added with a bitter edge to his voice. "It was all because I lived near the railway line and the canal."

"So! You see, do you — that you were tricked and used?"

"Brother," Thirza murmured reprovingly, but

Gottlieb was not to be swayed.

"To see one's self clearly can be the beginning of wisdom," he stated. "And how did Isaac become involved in this?"

"I sent him," Rebecca burst out. "I found Liam's note and sent Isaac and Alf Wister to rescue him."

"So," Gottlieb looked slowly around the table. "It would seem this man Alf Wister really is a government agent. Everything he said has come to pass."

"You should not have kept what he told you to yourself," Thirza stated firmly. "We are all involved."

"And until now why should I think my family is involved?" Gottlieb demanded testily. "He showed me papers from John Macdonald himself. They claim Wister is a government agent hunting Fenians, ferreting out — collaborators."

Liam's face burned as everyone deliberately looked away.

"Because we are close to Fenian targets, he stopped here. I told him we were not able to help him. My children, it seems, thought differently."

Rebecca met her father's ironic gaze unflinchingly.

"Well," Gottlieb continued, "that problem has been settled. We have now a problem of a different nature."

Master and apprentice regarded each other steadily. Liam wanted to say that he knew now he'd been wrong, about the Fenians, about Gottlieb — but before he could organize his words, Thirza interrupted.

"Brother, I must speak with you privately," she said firmly. "Rebecca, Liam, please go into the kitchen and close the door."

Liam stumbled to his feet and crossed the room. As Rebecca closed the door behind them, they could hear Thirza saying, "Gottlieb, this must not be decided hastily."

Liam stood awkwardly in the middle of the kitchen, glancing sideways at Rebecca.

"Perhaps tea would help," she suggested.

"I'll light the stove." Liam bolted for the back room that served as their summer kitchen and busied himself with wood and kindling, while Rebecca filled the kettle at the sink pump in the larder.

Back in the kitchen, Liam concentrated on picking cups from their hooks, aware of every sound Rebecca made rummaging among the tins of cookies and tea cakes. As he set a cup gently on the table, he realized they were both straining towards the parlour where the murmur of voices rose and fell. Gottlieb's low rumble was suddenly cut off as Thirza's voice came clearly through the closed door. "You are too demanding, Gottlieb. You must learn to be more tolerant of the mistakes of untried young men."

Liam plunked down the last cup and strode out onto the veranda. He was leaning against the wooden support trying to sort out his jumbled thoughts when he heard the clatter of wagon wheels. As Alf Wister's gaudy blue and yellow rig swung into their gravelled lane, Rebecca came flying onto the veranda.

"Run and tell them," she said breathlessly. "I'll keep him talking out here for a bit."

Liam turned furiously. "Will you stop..."

"I'm not being bossy, truly I'm not. We've got to give them time to decide what they're going to say to him." Her face puckered with worry.

"Sorry," he mumbled. He wanted to point out that Gottlieb was unlikely to stand up for him against a government agent, but when Rebecca said urgently, "Liam, please!" he turned back into the house.

He was just inside when Gottlieb opened the parlour door. Get it over with, he told himself.

"Sir, the scrapman, Alf Wister, has just pulled into the yard."

The master founder's face was expressionless. "So, the question is, why is he back, yes?" He raised an eyebrow at Liam, who nodded mutely. "Come." He strode through the kitchen. "We will find out." And Liam, still with no sign of Gottlieb's intentions towards him, followed nervously.

Alf was already up on the veranda and bounding towards the door with Rebecca scurrying after him. "G'day, sir, g'day." He stepped inside and pumped Gottlieb's hand. "Just dropped in with some news. Thought you might be innerested to know how our little bit of excitement turned out." His head bobbed from Gottlieb to Thirza, who had followed her brother out of the parlour. "And your son? Came through this dust-up all right, did he?"

"My nephew is quite safe, thank you, Mr. Wister," Thirza answered as she carried the large brown teapot to the stove where the kettle was just starting to whistle. "Isaac was involved in the fighting at Fort Erie, but he is back with us now — asleep upstairs. We must all be careful not to wake him."

"Just so, ma'am. Just so. Delighted to hear

no harm befell your household. Some others not quite so lucky, I reckon. Not as many as may be, thanks to the quick work of your two lads. Heard I caught up with a couple of cut-throats hereabouts, did yuh?" He was pulling out the kitchen chair Gottlieb had indicated while his eyes darted sharply from one face to another.

"Yes, we heard about the capture of these two men. And about the bombs." Gottlieb sat down opposite the junk dealer as Rebecca put a dish of butter beside the tea cakes on the table and Liam unhooked another cup from the china dresser.

"No, not two men," Alf corrected him. "One got clean away."

Liam almost dropped the cup.

"Got the important one, though," the junk-man continued. "Just in time, too. Cunning devil had already mined the bridge. I fixed that pretty smartly, I can tell you. Winkled it out as neat as a pin," Alf crowed. "Wunnerful con-traption, wunnerful. Would have blown that bridge up a treat! Took it apart real careful so's I could show it off later. No crackin' it up for kindling, like your young 'prentice there."

Liam looked away. Just stay out of it, he told himself, don't tempt him to ask any questions.

"How was he able to make such a thing, Mr. Wister?" Rebecca asked.

"Ah!" The blue eyes widened. "Found out all about him when we telegraphed down t' the States. Spent the whole war in the army, he did. Explosives expert. Once it was over, went looking for someone else who needed his talents. Hooked up with the Fenians. Plenty of money there. They collect from every Irishman in the States and plenty in Canada, too."

"Surely he did it because he's Irish," Rebecca protested.

"Bless you, miss, no. The likes of Fergus Whelan don't work for anything but money! Glad to get my hands on him, I can tell you. Couldn't check on the other one. Didn't know his name. Don't know where he got to."

Liam stared rigidly at the table. That wasn't a question. I don't have to say anything. But he could feel the silence as though everyone in the room were holding in breath.

Gottlieb cleared his throat. "I have told my family that you work for the government, Mr. Wister, hunting spies."

"Bet that surprised you, eh?" Alf grinned around the table. "Oh, don't you worry. I'm the genuine article when it comes to scrap metal. Got a real feel for sniffin' out prime goods.

That's what makes me so valuable to the government. I gets into places what gentlemen in top hats could never get into. And I senses things. Got a funny feeling the first time I run into young Liam O'Brien here, a real funny feeling. And once I'd passed that name around — the one on that parcel you delivered, young sir — well, what my contacts told me fair made my hair stand up on my head! Right glad to have a good excuse to call by here. When I saw the lay o' the land — railway line practically runnin' through the yard, canal no more'n a short spit away — somethin' told me to keep a good close eye on things."

Liam felt almost relieved. So he knew everything, this funny little man — and what he didn't know he could guess. So, what now? Am I to be herded off to jail? Ah, well, what does it matter? Get it over with! He took a deep breath and looked straight into the knowing blue eyes. "You're right, Mr. Wister, except that I was working with my cousin, Patrick, not with" — he all but spat the name out — "Fergus Whelan."

Before he could think how to continue, Gottlieb's voice broke in. "My apprentice was temporarily led into error by his kinsman. This man was a cousin, an emissary from Liam's family in Ireland and a persuasive talker. It is no surprise that a boy of fourteen should be tricked by such a one as this. We cannot expect to find old heads on young shoulders."

Liam heard Rebecca's sharp intake of breath.

"It would seem," the founder continued, "that he, in fact, made it possible for you to catch this man Whelan."

"Well, as to that, sir," the scrapman began ruminatively, "as to that — I wasn't far behind him. Not far. To be fair, though, to be fair, young Master O'Brien here certainly saved us all a couple of tarnation big blow-ups. What's more, it's none of my business to reel in the sprats. It's the big fish I'm after, and I reckon I got one of the biggest. One thing you might think about though, young master." He turned and spoke directly to Liam for the first time since he'd arrived. "There's precious little to choose between a patriot and a traitor. It all depends on who's holding the guns at the end of the battle." And as Liam was puzzling through that statement, the scrap dealer surprised them all by jumping to his feet. "Well, ma'am, I thank you kindly for the vittles. I'll be off on my rounds. Not much scrap dealing being done, I can tell you. But information — that little sideline's picked up nicely!" He tipped his cap to Thirza, winked at Rebecca and headed for the door with Gottlieb right behind him.

"Well!" Rebecca exclaimed as the kitchen door clicked shut. "Imagine that. Papa stood up for you, Liam."

"Don't rejoice too quickly," her aunt warned. "This means only that we have gotten rid of Alf Wister. Your father does not like outside interference in family matters."

CHAPTER

FIFTEEN

Liam started to stack the plates. *Whatever he says, I won't complain, if only he'll let me stay. Ah, wishful thinking, again! Why should he let you stay?*

"I'll take those!" Rebecca whisked the dishes out of his hands.

"Sorry." He stood out of her way as she bustled into the summer kitchen. He heard plates clattering, water splashing. *I should go and help.* Instead he stood numbly, thinking about his year at the foundry. *Face it, no matter what you thought, Gottlieb was fair. So he took you out of friendship for Da? What's so bad about that? Yes, he does lose his temper...but* you've had a place at his table, training in his craft. Shouting, yes... but never the flat of his hand or the toe of his boot. But now? What will he do? That first month I was here, he threw that apprentice out just for spoiling a pour.

Liam rubbed sweaty palms up and down the rough wool of his trousers. I want to stay, he whispered to himself. Isaac, Thirza, Rebecca — he pictured each one. These are my family. Yes, even Gottlieb.

The door swung open. The founder walked slowly across the room and sat down at the table. He looked at his sister, hovering between cupboard and table. "Wister will do nothing more about this. He was interested only in tying up loose ends."

"And so?" Thirza prompted.

"And so all we need now consider is how we feel about — these things which have happened."

"We must settle it today, brother," she said coming back to the table and sitting down. "We cannot live any longer with such tension in the house."

Liam sat down numbly. This is it — five minutes and it will be over. He was aware of Rebecca sliding into the chair beside him, felt her surreptitiously pat his hand but he couldn't even smile a thank you.

Her father, eyes fixed grimly on some point in the distance, began to speak. "My boy, putting aside family connections, the facts we know are these — you agreed to work as a spy for an invading enemy against whom we have had to defend ourselves at the cost of several lives. By great good luck, this household has not been touched — so far. There is no denying that you have done these things and they weigh heavily against you."

Liam could think of nothing to say except, "Yes, sir."

"What can we find in your favour to balance the scales?"

Liam pictured the huge foundry scales with its two large pans hanging from outstretched brass arms. All his misdeeds weighed down one pan. There's nothing, he decided dejectedly, nothing to put on the other side.

"But, Papa, smashing those bombs — helping to catch that man, Fergus — telling about the bomb under the bridge! Surely all that cancels out the rest! You said yourself they're his countrymen. And he did try to stop them!"

"Peace, daughter. Yes, it is true, actions show

the measure of a person. But there is also intent. And this I do not yet understand. Why," he asked, turning to Liam, "why would you do this? Have we not always tried to be fair, to treat you as one of us?"

Liam swallowed. His voice, when he could make a sound, was rusty with emotion. "I never thought...I...Patrick was family. Kin! He reminded me of...good times in my aunts' house...being with my father. I wanted...to do the things my father had done...back in Ireland."

"But, Liam," Aunt Thirza's gentle voice interrupted. "How many times did your father sit in this very room and say, 'I know now we cannot fight them. War only makes the hatred run deeper. We must change the way they think.' Surely you remember him saying that?"

Liam could look nowhere but at the hands clenched in his lap. How could he convince them that all his father's impassioned speeches had been blanked out by Patrick's honeyed words? "Yes," he admitted finally, "I do remember. But when Patrick first came ... it was such an adventure...and life here..." Liam stopped. How could he say out loud that he'd been restless and bored, fed up with hard work and being yelled at? His reasons seemed trivial, insulting. But even as he thought that, he knew he had to try.

"I know I was a disappointment to you in the foundry, sir. I…I didn't work carefully…the moulds were messy and…other things…" —he shrugged, struggling to remember details — "…were bad. I guess I thought it was all your fault. My father never yelled at me, but…" — Liam forced himself to look squarely at Gottlieb — "…he did expect me to do my best. I didn't do my best in the foundry. I realize that now. And even if I was feeling hard done by, that was no excuse for…" What else could he say?

"No," Thirza agreed gravely, "nothing can excuse what you did."

"I understand. I know I'll have to leave."

"No, I didn't say that," Thirza contradicted him. "I think you have learned something important." Liam looked up, hopeful for the first time in this difficult discussion. "And I, for one, am willing to forgive, even if I cannot excuse."

Liam, with tears stinging his eyes, felt Rebecca clutching his hand but it was Gottlieb he turned to.

The black eyebrows and enveloping beard hid all expression. Finally the master founder cleared his throat. His voice was harsh. "I ask much of you in the foundry because you have much to give. You are careless, yes, but you are not awkward or clumsy. You have it in you to be a good founder. If I am hard on you, well, good metal is forged in a hot fire. Is this not so?"

"Yes, sir."

"But this does not solve the harder problem." Gottlieb was silent again, eyes closed, head bowed, as the mantle clock ticked off the interminable seconds. Then he sighed. "We are told that to forgive is the highest virtue," he said as though arguing with himself. Then he raised his head and looked at Liam. "My son, I find it difficult to understand why you would associate yourself with such men." He paused. "But … I am willing to give you time to show us you can become the kind of man your father thought he was raising."

Liam stared at the founder. Another chance? He heard a whoop from the door and felt Isaac thumping him joyfully on the back.

SIXTEEN

Liam blinked awake. Sun up already! He rolled over and stretched. July 1, 1867 — Confederation Day. Today we ring the bell! Who would have thought, this time last year… His thoughts drifted back to those tense days — seeing Isaac back to the army camp, feeling guilty every time the word "Fenian" was mentioned. Well, at least that part was better once the Fenians moved east and started making a nuisance of themselves over by Kingston. Only a couple of months until the government gave up defending Niagara and Isaac came home. Of course the newspapers were still full of them. He couldn't understand the compulsion he'd had to search through the lists of captured Fenians. As though I cared... Still, it was a relief never to find Patrick's name. Perhaps he really did go back to Ireland.

Then there was the bell. The minute Isaac came home they'd started back at it. What a job that had been, shaping the upper part of the mould! Liam had stuck close to Isaac, carefully copying everything he did. Must have worked. There'd been a lot less shouting in the foundry. Mind you, Gottlieb had been preoccupied, trying to decide on the bell's inscription. Ordinary bells showed the casting date and the maker's name. But this was no ordinary bell — and a century from now, when bell maker and patrons were long since gone, its inscription must tell its story.

For weeks Gottlieb and a committee of township fathers pondered the problem. What should the bell announce about the event it commemorated? In the end, Aunt Thirza came up with the perfect inscription to encircle the sound bow. From a plaque on the wall of Britain's famous Whitechapel Foundry she borrowed the words: My voice shall go out to all nations.

Liam rolled the words over and over on his tongue, making music out of them. Then one day he found a phrase in a book of his father's that seemed almost a continuation of that thought, *Jubilate Deo Omnis Terra* — "Give praise to God all ye nations of the Earth." Hesitantly he read it out to the family after supper one evening. The next day he almost burst with pride as Gottlieb punched it, in mirror-image, onto the shoulder of the bell mould. Then two last inscriptions were fashioned into the mould: *G. Hahn me fecit*, A.D. 1867, and, to remind everyone of the reason for the bell,

God Bless Our Sovereign
Her Gracious Majesty Queen Victoria,
July 1, 1867

The mould was ready — and stood ready for two months! "Why not cast it straight away?" Liam asked, but all Isaac would say was, "I think he's waiting for something." And so it proved. In January the news flashed by telegraph around the countryside — the British Parliament had voted. Royal assent had been given. Canada existed!

"So," Gottlieb said, "today must the furnace be charged. Tomorrow we cast the bell." He never explained why he had waited, but Liam often wondered if he had been afraid to hex the bell by casting it before the fact. Bell founders respected the oddities of great bells and even practical Gottlieb told stories of eerie happenings on the days when important bells were being poured.

After a week of cooling, the bell had been unmoulded and turned mouth-up for tuning. At Gottlieb's first measured tap, the shimmering hum that vibrated through the casting shed proclaimed the bell a masterpiece. The final test would come with that first peal, when the great bell was rung to celebrate Confederation.

But it wasn't just the township bell that made this year special. On a shelf in the foundry sat six small but flawless bells, Liam's first casting since that disaster, almost eighteen months ago now. All thanks to Isaac — and not just for persuading his father. In working alongside Isaac, he'd learned to take pleasure from making each step along the way perfect.

He glanced across the room. Isaac was still sleeping. No need to get up yet. He was about to close his eyes when an insistent clanging startled him wide awake. Before he could react, Isaac leaped out of bed and threw open the window.

"Rebecca," he hollered over the clamour of

the dinner bell, "stop that infernal noise!"

"Then get up, you lazybones. Picnic today. Hurry!"

Liam spent the morning running up and down the cellar steps fetching jars and pots of preserves for Aunt Thirza to pack into baskets. On the veranda, Isaac sat polishing his boots to a mirror gleam while Rebecca put the last touches of the iron to his uniform. His artillery unit was to fire the Royal salute and Aunt Thirza was determined he would look perfect.

By mid-morning Isaac was in a frenzy to be away to the practice. He stood impatiently in the kitchen while Thirza and Rebecca brushed and patted and tweaked at him until his navy militia tunic sat perfectly across his broad shoulders and fell in knife pleats from his belt. Liam smiled as he watched Isaac tuck a rag into one pocket to dust his boots after the walk into Stonebridge.

At eleven the rest of them were ready to start off to town. They were all in new clothes — fine tweeds with checkered waistcoats for Liam and Gottlieb, white ruffled summer cottons for Rebecca and Thirza.

"Is everything in?" Thirza asked, as Liam settled the last picnic hamper in the back of the wagon. Rebecca picked her way gingerly down the steps, a large bowl in her hands. "Ah, here's the blancmange. Liam, you hop up there and hold this in your lap. It's too delicate to set down. Hand it up to him, Rebecca."

Liam hoisted himself onto the tail of the wagon and leaned down to take the bowl. Rebecca's face was tilted up to him, black hair swept up under a broad-brimmed hat. She smiled and his hands shook on the bowl.

"Come along, Rebecca!" Aunt Thirza called and Liam watched her run, with a swirl of white-ruffled skirts, to climb between her aunt and her father on the high-perched wagon seat.

The wagon started up with a lurch. As Liam sat clutching the bowl of pudding, he heard Rebecca and her aunt call greetings to neighbours streaming towards Stonebridge. Some were on foot, many on horseback with panniers of food strapped on the horses' sides and children riding pillion behind. Others, like the Hahns, had wagons full of family and food. They were looking forward to having the most fun they'd had in years, surpassing even the day the bell had been hung.

The closer they got to town the more Liam's mind turned to that bell. He had helped Isaac and Gottlieb finish the belfry on the town hall.

Then all the neighbourhood had turned out to hoist the two-hundred-weight of shining bronze into place. The bell had been hung mute, its clapper well wrapped in linen to prevent pranksters from ringing it prematurely. Even Gottlieb would not know the true sound of his bell until high noon, when it would ring out the news of Canada's nationhood.

As the wagon pulled past the town hall, Liam looked up at the belfry. A white lanyard ran from the bell's iron armature to a hook beside the door. Ready for the big moment, Liam thought as he set the bowl of pudding safely on the wagon floor. He jumped down from the wagon to help Aunt Thirza and Rebecca dismount. Rebecca, for once, waited until he had hauled out the portable wooden steps that made climbing out of a wagon in full skirts and petticoats less of an undignified scramble.

"Isn't it wonderful!" she exclaimed as she whirled her parasol in a dangerous arc towards the field teeming with laughing, darting merrymakers. A large square had been cordoned off beside the township hall for the military drill. At the far end was a raised dais festooned in red, white and blue. From a temporary flagpole behind it rippled a large Union Jack. Here the reeve of the township, Gottlieb and the local militia's commanding officer would deliver their speeches.

"Liam! I have for you a job." Gottlieb beckoned him over to the town hall. "In fifteen minutes will the ceremony start. I wish you to climb to the belfry and unshroud the clapper, then stand guard by the lanyard until it is time for me to ring the bell."

Liam looked at the founder. The black eyebrows and beard still made him look fierce but the voice sounded — almost warm.

"Thank you, Master Hahn."

Gottlieb glanced away with a small shrug. He's embarrassed, Liam realized as the founder muttered gruffly, *"Kletter schnell!* Climb quickly."

As Liam turned to dash up the stairs he heard Gottlieb call, *"Aber vorsichtig —* carefully!" Liam grinned and bounded to the top.

Five minutes later Liam was standing guard by the lanyard. No one, not even Isaac, is putting a finger on this, he promised, folding his arms and leaning with his back on the end of the rope. Gottlieb, the reeve and the township councillors were in place on the dais. The crowd stood three deep around the cordoned sides of the parade square. The band, deafeningly loud, marched down the centre of the square and wheeled to the right followed by the colour party flying regimental flags and the Union Jack. Stepping smartly behind came their own township regiments and the Welland Field Battery.

Suddenly Gottlieb was at his side. Over the noise of the crowd he motioned to Liam that he would take over. With a quick wave of his hand, Liam darted through the crowd to where Rebecca and Aunt Thirza had found places right against the rope barrier near the platform.

"Look, there's Isaac!" Rebecca pointed across the field as Liam squeezed in beside her. "Doesn't he look wonderful?"

"Wonderful," Liam agreed, but he was smiling at Rebecca.

A sudden blare of trumpets drew everyone's attention to the far end of the field. The reeve, a stout man, imposing in black with a new top hat for the occasion, stepped to the front of the dais. The crowd quieted. Liam could hear only the soft snorting of horses and the quickly quelled voice of a child as the reeve unscrolled the official proclamation.

Raising his voice so it carried down the field, he read out the words already familiar from posters and newspapers:

We, Victoria Regina, in the thirtieth year of Our Reign, by and with the Advice of Our Privy Council, have thought fit to issue this Our Royal Proclamation and We do Ordain, Declare and Command that on the First Day of July One thousand eight hundred and sixty-seven the Provinces of Canada, Nova Scotia and New Brunswick shall form and be One Dominion under the Name of Canada.

The reeve had no sooner shouted "God save the Queen" than the volunteers snapped to attention and fired off a deafening *feu de joie*. Then it was the Welland Field Battery's turn. Isaac and his comrades had polished the barrels of their field pieces so they shone like burnished gold in the summer sun. Stiff and smart in his navy uniform, Isaac stepped forward to pull the firing lanyard on the first gun. Then, one by one, the guns roared their salute to Victoria, Queen of the New Dominion, and the crowd matched the roars with their voices.

The tumult rose and rose as the last smoke from the guns trailed wispily and dispersed in the sultry breeze. Again the reeve held up his hand for silence. With a few last piercing whistles from rowdy boys at the fringes, the crowd quieted to a murmur.

"We celebrate this joyous occasion with our

own note of confidence in the future of this great nation — the ringing of our Confederation Bell. We thank all our neighbours for their generous donations but especially we thank our own bell maker, Gottlieb Hahn, founder in this community for many years and valued citizen and neighbour. I now call on Mr. Hahn to ring the first peal — after which, let the festivities begin!"

This is it, Liam thought, this is it. The crowd surged slightly and he braced his feet to keep Thirza and Rebecca from being pressed against the ropes. Rebecca smiled her thanks. Liam took her hand and tucked it under his elbow. Together they looked towards the Township Hall where Gottlieb stood on the steps. With slow deliberation, the master founder reached above his head, grasped the bell rope in those great, square hands and leaned lovingly on it.

Sonorous, deep and sweet, the bell's first peal rang out. Liam felt the sound quiver through him.

You were right, Da, you were right.

* * *

HISTORICAL NOTE

Liam and his father came to America, as so many immigrants did, to escape persecution and find the freedom to live as they wished. But they discovered that the new land had its own troubles. One problem was fear of the United States. For nearly one hundred years, Americans had been threatening to swallow the four small northern colonies of Nova Scotia, New Brunswick, Prince Edward Island and the United Province of Canada (now Ontario and Quebec). By the 1860s, Britain was beginning to grumble about the cost of sending soldiers out to defend that long, long border. The colonial leaders asked themselves what could be done.

"Unite into one large country with a federal government to look after defence," one faction said.

"Never," cried little factions in each colony. "We want to run things our own way in our own territory."

John A. Macdonald, a Kingston lawyer, tried to show the colonies the benefits of joining together. "One set of government buildings would save money," he argued. "One railway system would make trading easier and a big country would be able to maintain a strong army."

Macdonald had secret information that convinced him the colonies would soon have to defend themselves. As Minister for Defence for the Province of Canada, he had set up a system of spies to keep an eye on the Americans. His Commissioner of Border Police, Gilbert McMicken, had recruited men like Alf Wister to travel around the countryside and through the northern United States, picking up information. From 1860 to 1864, while the Americans fought their Civil War, these spies watched and listened for hints that the American government might try to invade the British colonies. By 1865 the spies had heard rumours that a group called the Fenians were forming in the

211

United States with the intention of attacking the colonies.

The Fenians were Irish rebels. They fought the wealthy English landlords who owned most of the land in Ireland and rented it out at high rates to peasant farmers. For generations, the farmers had used the wheat crop to pay rent and taxes and the potato crop to feed their families. Then, in 1846, a blight struck the potato crops. For three years in a row, half-grown potatoes turned black and rotted in the fields. No one could figure out where the blight came from or how to fight it. The result was mass starvation. People dropped dead in the fields, along the roadways, in the hovels they called home. Some of the better landlords tried to help. They offered food and free passage to America. Although many thousands did emigrate and made good in the new land, thousands of others died in the poorhouses set up by the government. Fear and anger spurred a group of men to revolt. Calling themselves the Young Irelanders, they formed a secret society to avenge injustice. Some disguised themselves in women's clothes and beat up the agents of land owners, justices of the peace and the sheriffs' men who evicted tenants who had fallen behind in their rent. Liam's father, who was part of this group, had to escape from Ireland when he was recognized as one of a band who attacked a justice of the peace. His nephew, Patrick Danaghy, joined the group of Irish rebels who formed in the United States.

This group called themselves "Fenians" after the legendary Irish heroes, the Sinn Fein. To carry on their fight to free Ireland, they collected money from the Irish in America. Some of this was used to form the Irish Brigade, which fought in the Civil War. As a result, young men like Patrick and Fergus became hardened soldiers. After the war, a group of Irish-American ex-soldiers tried to invade Britain. Their ship was captured at sea by the British Navy. The Fenians then turned to Canada. If they couldn't sweep the English from Ireland, some reasoned, they could at least strike a blow at the closest British possession.

The Fenians had spies roaming the Niagara Peninsula taking note of the best places to disrupt the communication systems. They planned to cut telegraph wires, blow up railway bridges and blow up the Welland Canal.

Fenian plans to invade the Peninsula were known to spies like Alf Wister and passed on to

John A. Macdonald as early as 1865. The strongest rumour said the attack would take place on St. Patrick's Day, March 17, 1866. John A. Macdonald called out the militia, young men like Isaac, to defend the Niagara frontier. Huge numbers volunteered and the government had trouble arming and training them all. The March 17 date passed with no incidents but the spies reported that the Fenians were still camping outside Buffalo and at other good border-crossing spots. Macdonald kept the militia in training all through the spring and early summer. Even so, the army was caught off guard when the Fenians finally crossed the Niagara River on the night of May 31, 1866.

Senior militia officers, none of whom had any battle experience, rushed their troops by train to the border crossing. By late morning of June 1, scouts reported that the Fenians had captured Fort Erie, cut the local telegraph wires, blown up some of the bridges and moved as far inland as Ridgeway. One trainload of militia set off from Port Colborne with their commander, Colonel A. Booker. They hoped that a second unit from Hamilton would meet them en route. They were out of luck. Alone on the farm fields around the village of Ridgeway, they met the oncoming Fenians. The battle was short and sharp. Both sides backed off quickly and the Canadian wounded were carried into a local farmhouse.

Meanwhile a small group of artillerymen set out from Port Colborne by lake steamer. They landed in what seemed a deserted Fort Erie but were caught by groups of Fenians returning from the battle of Ridgeway. By late evening the bulk of the Canadian army arrived from Hamilton and forced the Fenians back to the Niagara River. As they rowed themselves back to American soil on anything that would float, an American warship steamed out of Lake Erie and took them into custody.

The Fenian raid lasted less than forty-eight hours but Canadians were shocked to find how easily an invading army could march through their country. The Fenian attack changed the minds of many who had been hesitant about joining with the other British colonies in a Confederation. John A. Macdonald kept secret for many years another piece of information relayed by Henri le Caron, a British agent pretending to be a Fenian. At a meeting with Andrew Johnson, the President of the United States, the Fenian leader, Col. O'Neil, complained because the American Navy arrested Fenians as they crossed the Niagara. "I gave you five days," the president replied. "What more could I do?" To Macdonald and the British agent, this was proof that the American government leaders were willing to ignore their own Neutrality Laws if it seemed that a group like the Fenians might capture some northern territory for them.

Fenian scares continued for many years but none was as severe as the Battle of Ridgeway. In the meantime, the colonists prepared to celebrate the creation of a new country. In January of 1867 the British Parliament gave its official consent and Queen Victoria chose July 1 as Canada's birthday. To commemorate this special day, craftsmen like Gottlieb Hahn cast bronze plaques or bells, built stone cairns or erected township buildings.

July 1 was a hot, sunny day in 1867 — perfect weather for the celebrations. Communities in every corner of the new country held giant picnics where they roasted oxen, marched to military bands, set off fireworks and dedicated their own Confederation Day memorials. The newly knighted Sir John A. Macdonald became the first Prime Minister of Canada.